I'm Having His Baby Too

By

Author J. Cobbs

I'm Having His Baby Too

Copyright © 2023 by J. Cobbs

Published by Tyanna Presents

www.tyannapresents1@gmail.com

ACKNOWLEDGMENTS

I would love to say thank you to all my fans! I am very grateful for you guys allowing me to give you more of J. Cobbs. Lonnie, Kah'maycio. Kah'monie, Kah'leah, Kah'lonah and Kah'nari Cobb Mommy loved y'all. Thank you, Ms. T, once again for allowing me to show my talents. My pen sisters, Y'all up next! I Love y'all and let's put Tyanna Presents on the map. Mommy and daddy, your baby gurl did it! I know you're proud of me.

To keep up with me please follow me on Facebook @authorJcobbs.

Thank you!

Synopsis

Otis and Gail are married and have been forever, but after four kids, Gail is no longer the woman he fell in love with, nor does he desire her anymore. Deciding to get back to his old self, Otis shoots his shot with a baddie one day at a gas station. From that point on, he'll be in too deep. Will he make the biggest mistake of his life and lose his family? Or will he discover what he has before it's too late.

Gail Jones loves her family and wouldn't trade them for the world. Meeting Otis in high school and falling in love with him was the best thing that could have ever happened to her. Although she knows her image has changed, in her mind, her and Otis's love should be stronger than ever. Trying to make her husband love her isn't working anymore, but will Gail continue to try to make him see what he could lose?

ONE

Otis opened his eyes and looked around his kitchen. At the table sat his nine months pregnant with their fifth child. He looked at her and wanted to vomit. He hated how big she had gotten with this child, and just looking at her made him feel some type of way.

"Otis, I think we should have a night out. I want to hit a jazz spot and enjoy some good, soothing music," suggested Gail.

Otis sucked his teeth, then he walked over to the stove. He reached for the pot of rice and fixed him some and added condiments. Otis was a huge fan of plain rice with salt, butter, and black pepper added to it. He was not extremely hard to please.

"Who is going to watch the kids? Do you see your stomach? How much dancing can you do with all that popping out in front of you?" Otis asked.

Otis stood in his kitchen, looking at his wife. He was beyond tired of her asking for his time. Otis was not into having another child, and wanted no parts in what was baking in Gail's oven.

Otis Jones, twenty-nine-year-old born Georgia native. He was known around his small town of McIntosh as the heartbreaker. Before Gail swept him away, he was fucking and talking to every girl who walked in his path. He could not help it; he was addicted to sex.

Otis met Gail when he was just twenty-four with no kids. She was not supposed to have any kids, but somehow, it happened. Even though he hated being a father, he took care of his kids and made sure they were straight. He was not a dead-beat dad by a long shot and Gail knew this.

He spotted Gail at the Crab Shack. She was a waitress there, and he stepped to her while on a date with another chick.

"Aye, what is your name?" Otis asked the clerk.

"My name is Gail, and you want my name for what reason?" she replied.

Otis huffed, then smiled. He loved it when ladies tried to act snobbish.

"I am Otis. I just wanted to tell you that you have an amazing smile," Otis said.

Gail smiled. She loved the attention she was receiving from this stranger.

"Thank you so much. I hope your wife doesn't mind you giving me a compliment like that," joked Gail.

Otis's smile went away quickly.

"Wife? I am not married. The young lady I am waiting for is my sister," replied Otis.

Gail blinked.

"If you do not mind, can I get your number?" asked Otis.

"Sure," replied Gail.

Gail fetched a receipt from the front of her apron and jotted down her number, then she handed it to Otis.

The two of them had not stopped talking from that day.

"Can we go out before I have this baby? I have already talked to Shelia, and she will watch the kids for us, please," Gail pleaded.

Otis did not want to go out with his wife. He knew that meant hearing her complain about her feet hurting, back hurting, stomach cramping, and her being hungry. Otis was tired of hearing the same shit from his wife. He really enjoyed hanging out alone lately. It had gotten to where Otis would lie about staying late for work and hang out at the local bar.

"Say what? You already asked her?" questioned Otis.

Gail looked at her husband, then smiled. She loved the puzzled look on his face when he had no idea what she had done. She wanted time with her husband, and nothing was going her way.

Lately, Gail had been feeling like she was losing Otis, so she wanted to do as many things as possible before she had the baby to show him he mattered. The last two kids caused Otis to become distant, and Gail was not feeling it.

"Yes, I did ask her. As a matter of fact, I asked her Thursday at the supermarket. She asked me what day, and confirmed," answered Gail.

"Mommy, Tre will not share with me," a little voice said.

Otis turned away from the stove and looked at his son.

"PJ, you cannot expect Macho to play with you all the time," snapped Otis.

PJ stomped his feet, crossed his arms, and made the sourest face. He wanted it his way, and right now, but his father did not agree. PJ stormed over to his mom and reached for her to pick him up.

"Gail, you better not," snapped Otis.

She ignored her husband's remarks, leaned down, and picked up her five-year-old son. She loved all four of her boys. No matter how much of a stern voice Otis used, Gail did what she wanted when it came to her boys.

Gail gave birth to four wonderful boys named Kareem, who was seven years old, Josiah, who was six years old, PJ who was five years old and Alphature, who was three. Gail had her hands full with all these men.

"You still ignored what I said and picked him up, anyway?" asked Otis.

"What game you want to play? Maybe Mommy can play with you," Gail asked PJ.

"I want to color, and Kareem won't," wept PJ.

"Mommy would love to color with you," Gail said.

Otis rolled his eyes, then walked into the living room. As furious as he was, he just wanted some free time. He hated coming home from work, walking into his house, and seeing toys everywhere. He went and took a seat in his La-Z-Boy and grabbed the Roku remote. The last thing he wanted to do was color.

Swoosh!

An airplane sped by his face. He jerked back and

looked in the direction the plane jetted from. He saw his son, Alphature, standing at the room's entrance with a remote in his hand, and the biggest grin on his face. He wanted to play with his daddy.

"Damn, next time, warn me when you are coming for me," joked Otis.

He got up from the chair and raced toward his son. Alphature took off to the kitchen and dashed straight under the kitchen table.

"Whoa!" Gail yelled when she saw her son sprinting in the kitchen.

Otis was right behind him. He went down on his knees and followed his son under the table. Otis instantly started tickling his son, and play biting his arms and stomach.

"Mommy, you see Daddy eat Brother," PJ said.

Gail started laughing.

Otis got up from under the table, sat at the kitchen table, and leaned back in his chair. Alphature came from beneath the table and stormed off back toward his room. Otis reached for the spoon that was lying on the table, then he threw it toward his son.

"No, you don't," Gail said as she saw the spoon fly in the air.

"No, Daddy," PJ said while laughing.

Alphature trotted off so quickly, the spoon missed his fat head ass. Otis punched his fist together. He was mad he missed a perfect shot. He looked at Gail, then got up and reached for his keys on the keyholder.

"Where are you going?" asked Gail.

Otis turned around, holding up one finger.

"What is that supposed to mean? Where are you going, Otis?" Gail demanded.

Gail knew her husband had been acting funny lately, and wanted to make sure her heart was OK. Besides, she knew Otis had been working extra hard these past few weeks at Publix, so maybe that explained why he was acting so shady. Gail slowly got up from her chair, holding her stomach. She wanted to know where he was going.

"Is everything all right with us? You have been acting kind of distant with us," asked Gail.

Otis turned around, looked his wife straight in her eyes, and cuffed her face with the palm of his hand. She blinked and waited for her husband to make a move.

"Yes, we are OK. Why are you so worried? I told you this last month and the month before," Otis said as he kissed his wife's lips.

Gail embraced the kiss her husband gave her. It had

been quite a long time since she had an intimate moment with her husband.

Otis released her face after he kissed her. Gail reached out for a hug and Otis walked right past her open arms. He was not in a hugging mood, nor did he want to talk about their life in front of their son.

"What did I do? I am asking for a hug. Why are you being so damn mean?" Gail said.

"I am not having this conversation in front of my son. Can we talk later?" asked Otis.

Gail gave in to Otis's request and returned to her chair. She understood him not wanting to talk in front of their kids. They did not need to hear all the commotion.

Gail watched as Otis put on his Nike slides and walked out of their front door.

Gail sat there wondering what to do about her marriage. She was in love with Otis, but right now, he was giving her mixed signs. She wanted to fix whatever problem they had and fix it fast.

"Mama, we color?" asked PJ.

Gail stared at her son, then reached for a hug. He returned the hug with a tight squeeze and a wet, sloppy kiss on her forehead. She smiled.

J . C O B B S

TWO

Otis pulled into the Super Walmart shopping center and grabbed a parking space. He did not love shopping, but anything to get away from Gail. Otis sat in his 2019 Dodge Journey and looked at the shopping center. He really did not want to go to Walmart, but he did not want to go back home, either. Otis pulled out his iPhone and dialed a number. The phone rang.

"Hey, Tony. What is going on, crack baby?" joked Otis.

He reached for the button on the side of his chair and laid his chair back.

"Nigga, you know I'on smoke crack on Sundays," replied Tony.

Both laughed.

"Where you at?" asked Tony.

"I am on Scranton Connector at the Walmart," Otis said.

"Wait a minute, why the fuck you there?" asked

Tony.

Otis sucked his teeth.

"Brush them nasty bitches," Tony joked.

Both laughed again. Otis reached for his Black & Mild and lit it. He needed this to calm his nerves.

"Let me guess, you did not want to be at home with Gail?" Tony asked.

Otis did not answer right away. Instead, he hit his black. Tony already knew his homie was not feeling his wife anymore. But what he did not understand was why he was still there.

"Big homie, you know I love you like my brother, right?"

"I hear ya," replied Otis.

"Homie, why don't you just leave home? Why are you still there if you hate it so much?" questioned Tony.

Otis thought for a second, then hit his black again. Never had his friend asked him this question. When he replayed the question over in his head, he was puzzled. For once, he had an answer, but not the right answer. He puffed his black again.

"Honestly, I really do not know why I am still there. I mean, I know I hate the household," Otis said.

"Listen to yourself. I am not talking about the things

in your home, I am asking why you hate Gail?" Tony asked.

Otis blinked and stared in front of him. He was struck again, by yet another question he knew half and half.

It's because of the change in Gail's body that made me dislike her, Otis thought.

"Homie, I want you to hear me out," Otis said.

Tony rolled a blunt because he knew some bullshit was about to come.

"Listen, I got all day and time to talk to my brother," Tony said.

"I love Gail, do not get me wrong, man. But when she started having the boys, stuff was not the same anymore," Otis said.

"Look, come better than that," Tony shot back.

Otis sucked his teeth.

"She gained weight, the house is full of toys, pissy diapers, and baby shit everywhere. I am tired of coming home and not being comfortable," Otis snapped.

Tony's mouth was now on the floor, wide open. He could not believe what his friend had just said about his wife.

"Fool, did you say she gained weight? Are you fucking serious?" asked Tony.

Otis was dead serious and thought by telling his friend, he would understand. He made it worse by even mentioning this to his ass.

"Can I be serious with you? Yes, I can. Am I dead serious about her weight? Yes, I am," Otis said.

Tony lit the Kush blunt and started smoking. He did not want to come off as an ass, but he wanted to let his homie know he was dead ass wrong for feeling like that toward his wife.

"The woman you vowed to love and cherish, and now years later, you do not want her? Then you say it's her weight?" asked Tony.

Otis did not like how he made it sound. It sounded horrible.

"I am saying, she has gained some weight, and it has made me unattracted to her," Otis said.

"Come again?" asked Tony.

"My dick doesn't find her body attractive anymore," blurted Otis.

Tony could not even believe his ears at this very moment. What he wanted to say would only make matters worse. He was loss for words. He did not have a comeback line for that punch.

"Hello?" Otis said.

"I am here, shocked and loss for words," replied Tony.

"Let me explain more," Otis said.

"Please do," replied Tony.

"I am not in love with my wife like I was in the beginning. I have grown out of love with her looks and her style. She went and trapped me with all these kids, and I did not ask for them," Otis explained.

Tony saw where he was coming from now. It was not that he did not love Gail, he was dealing with stress. Tony went through this when Rayla had twins. He saw a doctor and they gave him medication to take. He spent about a year taking the medication and it helped him a lot.

"Bro, what you have going on has nothing to do with Gail. Do you recall how I acted when Rayla had the twins?" asked Tony.

Otis thought for a second.

"Dude, you were acting like you wanted to leave her ass. You even stayed with me for a small amount of time," Otis said.

"I was dealing with post partum depression. I think that's what the doctor told me," replied Tony.

Otis laughed.

He winked and thought hard about his homie.

"You may be right, but I know deep down inside, I do not want to be with my wife anymore. Shit is not the same anymore," Otis said.

"Why don't you just go home and talk to Gail? Even talk about going to see a doctor," Tony suggested.

"OK, I will talk to her. I am going home to tell her how I feel about us," Otis said.

Both sat on the phone and neither said a word.

Tony had nothing left to say about the situation at hand, Otis had to fix. No one else could. If he wanted to keep his family, he would get help. The ball was really in his court.

******

Gail loaded the kids into Shelia's car. Gail had told Otis they were going out this weekend, but because she felt like things were going bad, she asked Shelia to come over today.

"Thank you, Shelia, for coming on such short notice. I know I am late, but I need your help tonight," Gail said.

Shelia closed the door to her Ford Explorer and Gail walked back toward her house. Gail went inside and rushed to her bedroom. She went straight for the closet, pulled down her overnight purple duffle bag and huffed. She opened the bag and pulled out some candles and rose petals, and smiled. She raced back to the front door, then placed a line of red rose petals from the front door all the way back to her bedroom.

She then made a trail to their bathroom tub. Placing the stopper in the bottom of her all-white tub, she cut on the water. Gail turned around and reached for the "Axe Winterport" and placed three drops of it into the tub.

Then she reached for her phone that was on the bathroom countertop and sent out a text.

Hey, please come home. I am feeling sick and would like to lay down with you and watch a movie.

Gail sent the text to her husband, then folded her hands across her tummy. She stood there and looked at herself in the mirror. Gail shook her head, turned around, and walked out to their bathroom. She placed six candles on the floor, around the bed, and lit them, then walked over to her dresser and pulled out a red and black lingerie, two-piece set. She held the bra and panties up to her body, then shook her head.

She hated being so big and not being able to see her feet. She was ready to drop this baby and get her body back. She hated being a size twenty-two; that was not the woman Otis fell in love with.

Beep!

Her phone beeped with a new message. She reached for her phone and looked at the message.

OK, have you called the ambulance? I will be there shortly.

Gail smirked. She knew that meant she had time to get ready. Besides, she needed all the time she could get to prepare herself for the evening with her husband.

Gail thought about dinner.

What should I cook? Wait, cook? What? thought Gail.

She had not cooked for her husband in a while. Either the kids ate up everything, or mostly, she would order Door Dash for her and the kids. They were big fans of Door Dash and Uber Eats.

Gail lay across her bed and looked up at the ceiling. She yawned She realized her eyes were getting heavy. She blinked and tried to get up, but was stuck. She waddled to the right and then left and finally made it up.

She was tired. She leaned on her dresser to catch her breath. It was time to show Daddy some love!

Gametime!

THREE

"Touchdown!"

Otis rapped Yo Gotti's "Touchdown" as he pulled out of Wally World's parking lot. He was just about to go inside the store when Gail sent him a text, explaining she was not feeling good. He was not worried much because she still had some weeks left before she gave birth.

Maybe she just wanted me home.

Otis made a stop at the Quick Mart down the street from his house. If he was going home, he might as well grab him three packs of Game silver. He pulled into the parking lot and parked. He reached for his wallet and got out of his car. Another red Chevy Caprice on twenty-fours pulled beside his car, beating down the parking lot with Ball Greezy's "Nice and Slow".

Otis turned around and looked at where the music was coming from.

Otis bounced a little to the tunes. The driver's door opened, and Otis stopped in his tracks.

18

Damn, he thought.

Five-three, brown skinned, Cardi B body type, with long, brown hair. Her ass was like an overripe mango, just juicy. Otis looked at the young lady and his mouth dropped. He was amazed at her body.

When she turned and faced him, she said, "Well damn, take a picture, why don't you."

Otis opened the door for her and watched that ass as she walked inside the store. He went inside behind her. He went to the counter and waited to be called. The mysterious lady walked to the back of the store and grabbed a Pepsi from the cooler, then she walked to the snack lane. Otis watched every move she made.

"Aye!" the clerk yelled to get his attention.

Otis let the man behind him go first and waited for the hottie to come up. As the man walked by, he smiled. He knew what Otis was doing because he was watching the same ass in the store. The beauty walked down the aisle and went and stood behind Otis with a hand full of goodies. Suddenly, her sour cream and onion chips fell from her hands. Otis reached for the chips off the floor and held them for her.

The man who was in front of Otis went out the door, smiling.

Jacquees blasted through the front door when he opened it.

"Can I have my chips, sir?" the hottie said.

Otis smiled and put the chips behind his back.

"Only if you tell me your name and what kind of engine you have under your hood?" Otis asked.

She smiled.

When she smiled, she displayed dimples in both of her cheeks.

"Damn," Otis said.

Her dimples sent a feeling to his knees.

"Are you coming?" the clerk said.

Otis walked to the window, still holding her chips, and asked for his cigars.

"Can I get two packs of your Game silver?"

"Will that be all, my friend?" the clerk said.

Otis turned around and looked at the lady behind him.

"Go ahead and add your snacks, mama. I will pay for it," Otis said.

She smiled, walked past Otis, and placed her snacks on the counter, then backed away.

The clerk rang her snacks up and reached for the two packs of Game.

"Can you add two packs of Dutch honey to my bag, please?" she said.

Otis turned and looked at her, then waved for the clerk to add it.

The clerk did as he was told.

"Twenty-six dollars and eighty-four cents is your total," the clerk said.

Otis pulled out his Cash App card and paid for the order.

"Can I get your name? My name is Otis," he said.

He took his bag, turned around, and gave the hottie her bag. She took the bag, walked to the door, and went outside. Otis followed her.

She walked to her car, opened her door, reached inside and turned down her music. Then she put her bags on her seat and closed her door, turning to face Otis.

"My name is Gween, but call me GG," she said.

Otis smiled. He walked from beside his car over to Gween. He stood in front of her and reached his hand out for a shake. She shook his hand.

"Nice to meet you," Gween said.

Otis's eyes were glued to how beautiful her face was. Brown skin with not one pimple and nothing fake applied to her face. No fake lashes or any of the loud makeup Gail loved to wear. Her face was beautiful.

"I am," Otis tried to speak.

He was amazed by her appearance, he was now at a loss for words. He did not know what to say, but stuttered.

"Are you OK?" Gween asked as she laughed.

Otis stepped back and gazed at the beauty before him.

"A nigga just going to ask you, man. Let's match one?" asked Otis.

Gween smiled.

"I have respect for you, and I do not even know you. We can match one. Follow me to my spot," Gween said.

She turned and opened her door and went inside. Otis walked around to his car and got in and was ready to follow the hottie. She turned out of the Quick Mart and went down to Coastal Highway and made a right turn. Otis followed behind her like he was the police. She went down to the end of the road, made a left on Highway 341, right before the interstate. Then she turned right into the "Sixes Suites". She parked, got out, and waited for Otis to pull in beside her.

Otis pulled into the parking spot that was next to her car. He grabbed his cigar bag from his lap, and the zip of Kush he had in his glove box, and got out of his car. Gween stood there waiting at the end of her car, bent over the trunk.

Otis enjoyed the view. Gween saw him smiling and snapped her fingers. She leaned up and started walking to the front lobby of the hotel. Otis followed. Both walked through the front door and headed straight for the elevators. Gween pushed the up button and waited for the elevator to come down.

Otis's phone beeped with a message.

When you get here, please be quiet. I just put the kids down to sleep.

Otis looked at the message and frowned. His whole body tensed up. Gween saw his face and lowered her head. The elevator reached the fifth floor and it stopped. The doors opened and Gween exited the elevator and went to the right. She walked down to room five twenty-four and stopped. She reached inside of her bag and pulled out a gold hotel key and opened the door.

Both walked inside and the door closed by itself.

Gween walked straight to the bed and laid all her bags down. Otis looked around the suite as he followed Gween. He had never been to this hotel before. This one was brand new, and from the looks of it, this suite was hitting.

Gween sat on the bed and pointed for Otis to sit in the chair in front of her. He took a seat.

He looked around and saw three suitcases, clothes in the lounge chair, liquor bottles, lotion and other woman spays. He knew she had not been here too long. If he had to guess, he would say about a week.

"What is up? What made you come back to my spot with me?" Gween asked.

She grabbed a Dutch out of her bag and started breaking it down.

"I love what I see. You look like your interesting," Otis said.

Gween smiled as she started breaking down the weed in her Dutch. Otis grabbed his Game from his pocket, busted the pack open and grabbed a cigar out. He licked the cigar, then stopped when he saw Gween watching him.

"Damn, can I be that cigar you licking?" she joked.

She scooted back onto the bed and opened her legs. Otis tried not to focus on the pussy print that was playing catch me with him. Peeking through the navy-blue Nike tights, her pussy lips were fat as hell. It seemed as if she had a watermelon cut in two and placed on each side of her legs.

"You can be whatever you want to be," joked Otis.

He rolled the blunt, lit it, and slid back in the chair. He then looked at Gween, who was now looking straight at him.

"Tell me, are you single?" Gween asked.

Otis hit the blunt, passed his blunt to her and took hers.

"I have a wife," replied Otis.

Gween hit her blunt and choked. Otis was confused at whether it was because of the blunt, or him saying he had a wife.

"You are married? That is cool. I am not looking for a husband," answered Gween.

Otis smiled.

FOUR

Gail was finally dressed and had made her way downstairs to the living room. She plopped down in Otis's chair, all dolled up with her lingerie on. Gail had put on red L'Oréal lipstick number thirty-two with eye shadow. She was half naked, big belly all poking out of her shirt. Gail was feeling herself, and all she wanted was her man.

Gail looked at the last message she sent Otis and the time stamp. It had been almost one hour, and he had not shown up. Brunswick was not that far from McIntosh. It should take thirty minutes, max.

Gail looked at her call log and there was not one missed call from him.

Now she was worried. She did not know where to even start looking. She knew he was not at work, so where could he be? Suddenly, she thought about Tony and called him. She waited for him to answer.

"Hey, Sis," Tony said.

"Hey, Brother, Have you seen Otis?" Gail asked.

Tony knew his friend well, and nine times out of ten, he was back to his old ways.

"Yea, Sis, he is here sleep. We had a couple of beers," answered Tony.

Gail was upset and hurt. She wanted to surprise him, and it had been spoiled. A tear rolled down her face as she spoke to Tony.

"OK, thank you. I was worried," Gail said.

"What is going on with you two?" Tony asked.

Gail wondered why he would ask that. She wondered if Otis had said something to Tony for him to ask that.

"We are fine, why are you asking?" asked Gail.

Tony knew she was itching for some information, and he was not the one to give it up. Otis was his best friend, and he was not going to cross the line and tell Gail what he knew. His loyalty stood with Otis, not Gail.

"When he wakes up, I will tell him to call you," Tony said.

Gail hung up the phone and stared at the wall. She looked at the pictures of her and Otis, then turned to the kids's pictures. She was worried that her husband was cheating, and he was not. Gail took her time to stand up and looked at herself in her dresser mirror and spoke,

"You are a damn fool. You know Otis loves you."

Gail decided she would enjoy the bath since Otis had other plans. Gail waddled to the bathroom and started undressing.

****

Otis was standing with his dick out, looking at Gween. Gween was laying down on the bed, butt naked, legs spread wide with her fruit salad looking back at Otis.

"You sure this what you want?" Gween asked.

Before Otis could answer, Gween inserted two fingers into her pussy.

"Mmmm!" Gween moaned.

Otis stroked his dick one last time, then he removed her hands from her pussy.

"Wait, Daddy!" moaned Gween.

Otis took his time and kneeled down and started kissing her inner thighs.

"Stop! Stop! Wait, please!" moaned Gween.

Otis stopped kissing her thighs and placed his hard dick right on clitoris, He stroked her slowly and looked her straight in the face.

"You enjoy that?" Otis whispered.

Gween enjoyed the foreplay he gave her. With

every stroke he gave her pussy, she became wetter.

"Do you have a rubber?" asked Gween.

Otis stopped stroking and then stood up. He looked at his wallet in the dresser and knew he did not have any. He had not stepped out in a while, so there was no use for him to grab any like he used to.

"I am not going to lie; I do not have any. I do not step out like this, ma," replied Otis.

Gween sat up, naked, then she looked at Otis. She wanted that big, brown dick that was staring at her. It looked like a car she wanted to test drive.

Gween rose from the bed and stood in front of Otis. She placed his right hand on her left nipple, then put his left hand on her pussy. His eyes closed; he started playing with her pussy. Gween reached in and tongue kissed him. Otis returned the tongue kiss.

Gween twitched and could no longer stand still. The friction from Otis rubbing her pussy sent an electric wave through her whole body. She shook; Otis grabbed her and held her up with one hand and used the other one to drive her crazy.

Suddenly, Gween nutted all over Otis's hand.

Otis laid her down on the bed, then he climbed on top of her. Slowly, he kissed her neck and she moaned. Otis enjoyed all the energy Gween gave him. His dick was so hard, he was shocked. His dick had never gotten this hard for his wife. This new hardness was something like a brick of steel.

Otis slowly entered Gween's empire of wetness. She moaned.

Otis started kissing her neck as she moaned. Otis did not even want to dog her, he just wanted to put the head in and make her beg.

Otis leaned up, pulled her legs to his shoulders, then looked at her pink clit. Otis took his thumb and rubbed her clit in a circle. This made Gween go wild.

"What are you doing?" Gween asked.

Otis ignored her and slowly stuck his dick in her pussy.

"My God!" moaned Gween.

The impact of his hard dick jabbing her insides made her go wild. She grabbed Otis's back, then she clawed him. Otis felt her scratch him and this sent him over the bird nest. One thing he loved and missed was Gail scratching his back, biting him, and making him feel appreciated.

"You like that?" Otis asked.

Gween could not answer the question, because at

this moment, Otis grabbed her legs and was now long stroking her. He went so deep that, for a split second, he felt the bottom of her inside. He pushed but could not go any further. Gween moaned louder.

"Where you want me to…" Otis mumbled.

Before he could ask her where she wanted him to go, it was too late. Otis exploded inside of Gween's pussy. He shook; she moaned louder as he beat her pussy up. After six long jabs, it was over.

"You good?" Gween asked.

Otis placed her legs down and stepped back, catching his breath. Then he picked up his boxers and the rest of his clothing and walked off toward the bathroom. Gween sat up in the bed and watched him. She smiled.

Gween was feeling this man, but not like that. She was amazed at what he had just done to her body. The way she wet the bed and his chest made her smile. It had been a while since she'd had a one-night stand.

She got up from the bed and then walked to the bathroom door and knocked.

"Yes!" Otis yelled from behind the door.

"You need any help in there?" she asked.

"I got this, just make sure you change your sheets," joked Otis.

31

Gween grabbed her face. She could not believe he said that. She turned and looked at the bed. The spot was so big in the bed, it covered most of the queen bed. She raced over to the bed and started pulling the sheets off the bed. Then she saw the mattress was also wet. She could not bring herself to believe she had done that.

FIVE

Otis was now sitting in his car in his front yard with a big ass smile on his face. He looked and saw that Gail's car was still parked on the side. It did not look like she had gone anywhere. She was in the same position as before he left.

Otis reached for his phone and turned it on. Once he was chilling with Gween, he turned off his phone, and that was it. He did not care if any emergency happened, he was off the meter.

Otis looked at all the incoming text messages from last night. He was not bothered by any of them. The only message that made him smile was the one from Gween.

Hope you made it home safe. I had so much fun! Text me next time you are in the Wick. We have to hook up again.

Love Ms. G

Otis smiled so hard, his lips cracked just a bit. He

finally had that spunk back that he missed so much. She was sexy as fuck and just his type. For a split second, Otis totally forgot all about him being married. When he saw Gail standing at the front door, he blinked. He was startled, and wondered if she had seen him read the text and smile as well. He immediately opened his car door and headed toward the house.

"Are you OK? I have been calling you all night, and not one time did you answer," bugged Gail.

Otis ignored his wife, brushed past her and went inside his house. He had a great morning, and she was not going to ruin it.

He went inside and plopped down on his chair. He was tired and worn out. All the stroking he did like he was young, now his body was paying for it.

"Are you OK? How much did you drink?" Gail asked.

Otis rolled his eyes and laid his head back on his black leather loveseat. He did not have the energy to fuss with Gail, he just wanted to sleep. He had already showered at the hotel, so the woman's scent was washed off already. He was not worried about anything at the moment, not even his kids. He was happy from what had taken place earlier.

"I had a long night, I am tired," replied Otis.

"What if I had gone into labor? I would've just had to wait until you were done drinking and slept it off before I even heard from you?" Gail asked, throwing her hands up.

Otis was extremely mad now. He did not want to fuss with her, especially when his kids were home.

"Where are my kids? Why I do not hear them running and tearing up my shit?" snapped Otis.

Gail rolled her eyes, then took a step back from her husband. She looked at him up and down, then took another step back and grabbed her face. She saw marks on his neck, and Gail knew she had not put them there, or had she?

"Who is she? Is she at least sexy?" Gail asked.

Otis stood up, grabbed his cell phone from his back pocket and dialed a number.

"Who are you calling? Why are you calling her?" asked Gail.

Otis did not answer his wife. Instead, he looked at his phone as it kept ringing.

"Hello?"

"Hey, what's going on?" Otis asked.

Gail sat back in the chair. She knew who he had called and was not worried anymore. She just wanted to make sure it was not like how they met.

"I am home and Wifey is asking where and who I

was with last night. But you know where I was at last night and who I was with, correct?" asked Otis.

Tony let out a laugh.

"Look, man, if she does not believe you, then that is just her luck. Gail called me last night while you were passed out," answered Tony.

Otis turned and looked at his wife.

"Thank you," Otis said and hung up his phone.

Otis walked past his wife and gave her the dirtiest look, then headed for his bedroom. He did not have anything left to say to her at this point. It was plain and simple that she did not trust him, and he did not care.

He was not about to blast himself about last night. If she did not have any proof, it was nothing.

Otis got halfway up the stairs and turned around and noticed that the house was incredibly quiet. He did not see any blue-eyed kid hiding to shoot him, and nobody was crying either. He stopped, turned around, and yelled down to Gail.

"Where are the kids?" Otis asked for the second time.

Otis waited for his wife to reply. He paused in his tracks and stood there, waiting.

Gail rolled her eyes, then she waddled into the

kitchen to start her meal prep. She was making her famous Brunswick stew with cornbread.

Otis shook his head and went straight for his bedroom. He did not want to fuss with her. After the night he had, he only had energy to sleep.

Gail stood on the stairs and folded her arms.

Maybe he is being honest. Why am I jumping to conclusion? I am pregnant and my hormones are all over the place. He only cheated once in the beginning and that was when we had no kids. He works and pays the bills, plus he makes sure we do not want anything. Why am I trying to tear down my family?

Gail walked over to the mirror that was on her living room wall and stared at herself.

Look at how big I have gotten. My face is blacker than before. Oh my God, look at these bumps on my face. Where did they come from? I am using cream daily on my face. Gail looked at her face.

Feeling unpretty, Gail walked into her kitchen and sat at her sunflower table. She looked around the kitchen and then dropped her head on her table. She was not in the mood for cooking at this point; all she wanted was to feel sexy. Gail picked her head up from the table and looked down at her belly.

"Just one more week, and Mommy will have her body back," Gail whispered.

Gail pulled her cell phone out and scrolled down to "Desire" and pressed call.

If anyone could cheer her up, it would be her best friend of six years.

"Hello, baby," Desire said.

Gail laughed, then slid her chair out a little more from the table.

"I am OK. I just need a girls's day. I know you all wifed up, but can I steal my best friend for an hour or so?" Gail asked.

Desire laughed.

Gail got up out of her chair and walked toward the deep freezer. She wanted a "Lazy Boy" ice cream sandwich.

"I mean, we can go out today if you want to. Is Otis watching the kids?" asked Desire.

"Naw, they with the sitter until later today, so right now will be a great time to go out," replied Gail.

Desire agreed.

"OK, let me get ready and then I will meet you at Nail Us in the Publix shopping center. The one right off Highway 17," Gail said.

"OK, see you there," Desire said.

Gail looked down at herself. She knew going to tell Otis she was leaving did not matter. He did not care; not like he was going to ask where she was going, anyway.

Gail walked into her living room and fetched her keys and purse from the stand by the door. She turned and looked upstairs.

She wanted Otis to run down and ask her where she was going. After a few seconds, she walked out of her house. A tear fell down her cheek as she walked off her front porch. Gail was devastated that her husband did not care if she was in the house or not.

SIX

Otis was outside of his job, in his car, on his fifteen-minute break. He was parked in the Publix pickup service spot for members only, but he did not care. There was no parking on the side of the building where associates were supposed to park. Otis had been working for Publix for over ten years and was a shareholder and the highest paid assistant back house manager they had at his store. He hated working here, but without his job, bills would not be paid. Sleeping on the streets with his kids was not going to happen. He had overstayed his welcome at Publix. The long nights and over time had put some wear and tear on his body. He was the only one working in the house, so that meant he had to work. Gail was a stay-at-home spouse and hadn't had a job since she gave birth to their second child.

Otis turned his head and scanned the parking lot to see if he saw any of his coworkers. He was having a nicotine fit. Somehow, he left his fresh pack of Newport's in his dresser. He bit every nail he had, and now was on his

40

bottom lip. He did not see anybody he could ask for a Newport and that made him madder than he was. He knew there was a Parkers gas station right behind his store, but he did not want to move.

Otis was about to get out of his car when his phone rang. He looked down at the phone in his lap and shook his head. He knew who it was before he even looked down.

Why is Gail calling me? I just left her ass home this morning and came to work.

Otis got out of his car, pulled his sweater over his Publix apron, then answered his phone.

"Hello?" answered Otis.

"What took you so long to answer me, baby?" Gail joked.

Otis was not in the joking mood, nor did he want to talk to his wife at the moment. Lately, anything that involved Gail turned Otis off. He was just there and was trying to find out why.

"Look, I am at work! Did you have the baby?" Otis snapped.

"Honey, what is the matter with you? Why are you acting all mad and hostile?" demanded Gail.

"I am at work, tired and hungry as hell!" yelled Otis.

Otis was about to head to the pedestrian walkway when he stopped right in the middle of the street. In a parked car with their flashers on was Gween, sitting in the driver's seat. Otis stopped immediately, turned around and faced the way of the car and stared. He was shocked at who he saw. Otis was about to head toward the car when he saw a guy come out of Publix and hop in the passenger seat of the car. Gween then turned her flashers off and pulled off. Otis stood there.

HONK!

Otis jumped. He turned and saw a car was behind him, waiting for him to maneuver across the street. Otis walked in front of Gween's car and she stopped. Otis glanced inside of the car and looked Gween in her eye, then headed across the street.

Gween was shocked. Her mouth quickly dropped and then closed. She honked her horn for Otis to hurry across the street and she went on her way.

Otis stood on the sidewalk and watched the car drive down to the end of the parking lot, watched her as she went to the turn lane and left the parking lot.

Otis was hurt that she did not even stop to say hi.

"Hello!" yelled Gail.

Oh shit, I totally forgot I had her on the phone.

"Hey, sorry, I was crossing the street and almost got hit," replied Otis.

"Baby, are you OK?" asked Gail.

Otis entered the store and was ready to get these last four hours over with.

"My break is over. I will see you when I get off," Otis said as he hung up.

Otis went to the back of the store to the loading dock. A truck had just arrived before he went on break and now, he had to finish what the other guys hadn't unloaded.

Otis finally made it to the loading dock and dropped his head. This was a meat truck and the meat department had nobody to come and help with the inventory. Everyone decided to call off today, so that meant Otis was to unload the produce and the meat truck.

He grabbed his Publix jacket from the wall, then slowly walked over to all the pallets that were scattered all around the back house. His mind was not at work anymore. Otis wanted to see Gween.

After the first night they had, they only exchanged a few texts, nothing major, and that bothered Otis. He was ready to meet and get the party started. Otis moved slowly to start the truck.

***

"Girl, tell me why I seen Mr. Big Dick when I was picking up Flo from the store," Gween said.

Gween had finally made it back to her hotel room and was now running her mouth to her homie, Cat.

"Wait a minute. Did he say something to you?" asked Cat.

Gween laughed as she finished rolling her blunt in the Game diamond cigar. She licked the ends to fold it. She slid the whole cigar down her throat to get it wetter.

"What can he say? I sped right past his ass, and did not blink my motherfucking eye once," joked Gween.

Both ladies laughed.

Gween was not seeing anyone, but that still did not mean when she saw you in public she had to speak.

"When you going to see him again?" asked Cat.

Gween hit her blunt and waited for a few seconds before she gave a reply.

"Bitch, see him for what? Let his mind wander a little bit as to why I didn't stop and speak," answered Gween.

Gween loved playing games with niggas. Most of the stuff she had either came from her playing with a man or she stole it. Her hands were faster than anybody's eyes.

"You going to Billy's tonight?" asked Cat.

"You know your girl is going to be in the place, especially if Mrs. Queen love transportation going to be in the building! I love her company and her drivers," answered Gween.

"What are we wearing? I still have my jersey set we got from Gorgeous Minks, Queen Love transport is the shit, baby girl got her company and took the fuck off in the business." Cat said.

Beep!

There was a text coming in. Gween looked and saw it was from Otis. She smiled and clicked on the message.

Can we meet up later? If not, it is OK. I saw you today.

Gween did not even reply. Instead, she ended her conversation with Cat and got ready to get her nails done. It was her spa day, and nobody was getting in the way of her personal time.

SEVEN

It was a dry and sunny Friday afternoon and Gail refused to miss another spa day. Her feet were terrible. They looked like she wore no shoes. All the dead skin that had accumulated on the bottom and sides of her feet made her feel ugly. Never had she missed a spa day, but lately, it seemed like whenever it was time to go, she was tired.

After taking a shower and seeing her feet, it made her call up her stylist, Nay, and get a quick walk-in appointment.

Gail made her way to Brunswick so she could meet Nay at the shop. Gail sent a quick text to her babysitter to check on her youngest.

Hey, how are things going? Is Jr. OK?   I will grab him right after my last appointment.

Gail sent the text and pulled off. She wanted to hear from Otis, but lately, stuff had not been going like she planned. Gail wanted to spend time with Otis, but with him working two jobs, it was hard to find the right time. Either he was tired, or when he was off, he was with Tony.

Gail pulled into the Lanier shopping plaza off Club Drive. She saw Jerk Shak and wanted to stop immediately. For some reason, every time she came to Brunswick, she stopped by the Jerk Shak and grabbed a plate of chitterlings. It was her favorite food to eat, she just could not cook it like George and his crew did. Jerk Shak was famous for all their custom island dishes and great taste.

Gail got out of her car and waddled her way over to Nay's shop. It was now six thirty-three and the sun was just going down. The weather was muggy, with a stale fragrance. Brunswick, Georgia, always smelled like rotten ass, no matter what time of day you were out.

Gail walked up to the neon door with the word "Nay's" in fire pink. One thing Gail loved was how clean Nay's spot was. She picked a great spot to open her business. She was in the middle of a huge shopping complex. This meant more clientele for Nay.

Gail opened the door and was shocked. There were eight chairs in the salon and all of them were full.

Why would she tell me to come by if she had a full house?

Gail went and took a seat in the sitting area and waited to see her girl. Gail took out her phone and started watching TikTok clips. She might as well laugh while she waited for Nay. Beside the shop was stale and muggy. Only about three ladies were talking, and the rest were on their phones.

"Aye, man, what are we doing tonight? It is Friday night, so let us hit the streets," a lady said.

"I don't know about you, but I am shacking up with my married man," another lady said.

Gail bounced her head from her phone and looked in the direction of the two ladies talking. She heard married man and instantly looked around. Gail hated when sloppy women preyed on married men. She knew this scene all too well, being that her father cheated on her mother dozens of times.

"Gail," Nay said, coming from the back of the salon.

Gail heard her name being called, got up from the chair, and headed toward Nay standing in the back of the room.

"Hey there, friend," Gail said.

Eboni pointed to the chair next to the ladies who were talking. Gail took a seat and placed her black and red Gucci purse under her chair. Then she slowly slid closer to the table.

"I see we are almost at the finish line," joked Nay.

Gail laughed.

She knew Eboni was referring to her belly. The last time she was there, she was three months pregnant. Her stomach was not as huge as it was now.

"Yes, I will be so happy to get my life back!" replied Gail.

"Repeat that shit again," the lady to the left of Gail said.

Gail turned and looked at the two ladies at the booth next to her.

"Lady, I can tell by the way you walk, you are tired. You so over that pregnancy, it is written all over your swollen face," the dark-skinned lady said.

Gail laughed.

"My name is Gween. Sorry for butting in your conversation, but honey, I pray for you," Gween said.

Her homegirl next to her smiled. They both had no kids and really did not know what Gail was going through, but by her face, they could tell she was over it.

"I am very over this pregnancy. I am tired of the late-night hungriness, tired of being swollen, but most of all, I miss fucking my husband!" Gail said.

Both ladies and Nay looked at Gail. She was now in

49

tears. She did not mean for it to come out like that.

"Say what? You ain't getting no dick? You married?" Nay asked.

Gail laid her hands out for Nay to begin on them. She turned and looked at Gween and waited for a reply.

"Excuse me! So, not only are you pregnant, but he not even supplying you with the wood?" asked Gween.

"That is why you get you a nice lil friend," Nay said.

Gail wiped her eyes.

"I don't cheat."

"Honey, I never said cheat," Nay said.

"If you are not talking about cheating, then what are you saying?" Gween asked.

Gail listened carefully at this moment. She did not understand what Nay was talking about and wanted to know. Gail wanted her husband to be more romantic with her; she hated being the ugly duckling. All Gail wanted was some attention and affection from Otis.

"Honey, you are pregnant, you do not need to be 'round here, trying to have fun with anyone but your husband. What I am referring to is a sex toy!" Nay said.

Gail grabbed her face and giggled.

"A sex toy will not do you right! You got to get that

real heat from the dick," teased Gween.

Everybody laughed.

Gail knew all too well about sex toys. She had her own special get right bag filled with goodies. Since Otis had been acting all shitty and did not want to touch her, she had been using them. Gail had the rabbit, rose, ass plugs and the nipple licker. Gail had invested over three hundred dollars in sex toys. Still, none of them had even come close to Otis's touch and the feeling she got when he was inside of her.

Nay looked at Gail and shook her head.

"I have been doing your nails for over two years, and honestly, mama, you need a break," Nay said.

Gail looked at her stylist and knew she was right. All she had done since she had known Nay was complain about what Otis was not doing and her feelings.

"Honey, you been having a problem with your man for over two years and you still there?" Gween asked.

Gail knew it was stupid of her to lie, but why lie? She needed to hear someone else's point of view.

"I love my husband. The way we met was weird."

"How did you meet?" interrupted Gween.

"He was with his girlfriend, eating at my job. He approached me and asked me for my number, and his smile made me say yes," answered Gail.

Nay looked at Gail and opened her mouth.

"Wait a second, you never told me he had a bitch," Eboni blurted out.

"I am with you, Mrs. Nay. So he had a wife," chimed in Gween.

Ring!

Gail's phone rang. She looked at her phone and smiled. She was saved by the call.

Finally, he called me back.

"It must be him calling," Gween said.

Gail quickly put her phone to her ear.

"Hey, baby!"

All three ladies looked and listened to Gail's conversation.

"I know you were busy, that's why I sent the one text," Gail said.

Gween kicked her friend Resha, who was sitting next to her. She had been on her phone the entire time, not paying their conversation any attention.

"Otis, you do not have to get mad at me for that. I was just checking up on you, that is it," pleaded Gail.

Gail got heated and got up out of the chair. She stood up and looked at Nay, then she shook her head, grabbed her bag from the floor and made a dash for the front door.

Gween looked at Resha and then at Nay.

"Can I take her spot then since she just up and left?" asked Gween.

"I only made an exception for her because she is pregnant," replied Nay.

Gween rolled her eyes.

Nay got up from behind the nail booth and went in the back. Gween followed her with her eyes. Once she was out of sight, she looked at Resha.

"Did that hoe say Otis?" asked Gween, eyeing the ladies.

Resha dropped her head and then lifted it back up.

"Best friend, I do believe that is the name the hoe said," Resha confirmed.

Gween just leaned back in her chair and stared at the wall.

One thing a fuck nigga not going to do is play with me.

EIGHT

"It is all good, get your nails done. I am about to head over to Timothy's hotel. He is only in town for two days," Otis said.

Otis stood in the middle of his bedroom floor. He had just taken a shower and was putting the final changes to his outfit.

"Baby, I am leaving now. I can meet you at the house," Gail replied.

Otis knew his wife was going to try to meet him at home, so he thought of what to say fast. He already had plans and they did not include Gail.

"What did I say?" asked Otis.

He sucked his teeth and hung up on his wife. He grabbed his black and red Retros from beside his bed and took a seat on his bed. He was not worried about Gail coming home now. He had already been home for over an hour now. Otis played this Friday afternoon smart. He had been off work for more than an hour now and came home, took a shower, and made himself something to eat. When he was just about ready to step out the door, that was when he called Gail.

Otis had already made plans to hang out with Gween tonight. So, Gail trying to get him to stay home with her was out of the question. Otis was ready to see Gween again, the woman he really wanted to cuddle with.

Otis laced up his shoes and reached for his red and black Nike hat. He turned around and faced himself in the mirror and examined himself again. He looked up and down at his body in the full-length body mirror that hung from his wall. Gail loved mirrors. Every room in their house had one hanging somewhere.

For me to be almost forty, I must say my body damn sure still got it.

Otis laughed.

He grabbed his cell phone and made a dash downstairs to take the food out of the microwave. Otis went into the kitchen and started the dishwasher since he was cooking and making a mess. Then he went to the microwave and pulled out a plate with foil paper on it. Otis then placed the food on the kitchen table beside a card.

Otis took a step back, then exited the kitchen. He wanted Gail to feel happy when she got home, so he left her some grilled salmon and dirty rice. Otis picked up one of those "ready cook" meals for two from Publix. All he had to do was put the plate in the oven, then warm the rice in the microwave and he had a very quick and simple meal that took less than fifteen minutes.

Otis walked out of his front door and locked it, then he turned around and made his way to his car and got inside and started the engine. Otis checked his email quickly to make sure he had his confirmation number for the hotel he booked. He found the email and then put the address in his GPS. He sat there and rolled two blunts, then he turned on Boosie and backed out of his driveway. He was ready for tonight and wanted nothing to do with Gail or anything that involved her. He wanted free time away and that was exactly what he was doing.

Otis looked down at his gas needle and saw he had half a tank of fuel. He knew from McIntosh to Savannah would be about thirty minutes if the highway was not packed. Otis decided he did not need any gas for his ride.

As he pulled out of his neighborhood, he stared at the houses as he passed them. They had come a long way from Brunswick's projects. The life they had now was wonderful, except for one thing.

Otis's phone rang.

He looked down and saw Gail was calling. He
ignored the call, lit his blunt and made his way to Interstate
95, heading toward Savannah, GA. Hilton Resort was
calling his name, and the last thing he wanted was for his
wife to ruin his night. Besides, he stayed home last night,
so tonight, he got to run the streets.

****

"Hot girl got a date, I see?" Resha joked.

Gween walked out of the bathroom. She stood in
front of the mirror, admiring herself. The duo had spent
their weekend in Savannah, Georgia. Besides, Otis had
texted her earlier and told her he was getting a room at the
Hilton and wanted to spend some time with her. Gween
was not about to turn down a weekend at the Hilton paid
for by somebody else. Gween packed her overnight bag,
grabbed Resha, and they tore 95 North up.

"A date with who? I told you we came to have fun,"
Gween said as she sprinted back to the bathroom.

Wham!

Gween slammed the door. Resha jumped up off the
bed and trotted to the bathroom door.

"Are you OK in there?" Resha asked from the door.

She waited for a reply from Gween. After a few

seconds of not replying, she swung the door open.

Gween was on her knees, hugging the toilet. Her head went up and down in the toilet.

"Bitch!" yelled Resha.

She waited for Gween to get done and watched as she lay back against the bathroom wall. She pulled her hair back in a ponytail, then she wiped her mouth.

"Tell me you are not," blurted Resha.

Gween gave Resha a fucked-up look, then she got up off the bathroom floor. She walked over to the sink and cut on the faucet. She let the water run in her hands, then she splashed some on her face. She reached for the bathroom towel and dried her face.

"Are you going to answer me or you going to act like you and I both don't know what is going on," joked Resha.

Gween rolled her eyes and pushed past her, out of the bathroom. She went and laid on the bed. Gween rolled over and stared at the ceiling.

"Whose baby, G?" Resha asked as she lay next to her bestie.

Gween was not about to talk about a damn baby. She did not want a baby. What would she do with herself?

"My period is weeks late. Yes, I know I fucked up

this time," Gween said dryly.

Resha stared at her friend with her mouth wide open. She could not believe what her friend was telling her.

"Say what? Not Ms. I do not want a child," Resha said.

Gween was mad at herself right now for even opening her mouth. She knew the backlash her friend was going to give her was not something she wanted to hear.

"Tell me it is not that married man you been fucking with?" Resha asked.

Gween rolled over and faced the wall.

Resha took that gesture and knew what her answer was.

Suddenly, Gween's phone rang.

Gween jumped up and reached for her phone on the TV stand. Resha got up from the bed and went into the bathroom.

"Hello?" Gween said.

She looked behind her to make sure Resha was in the bathroom.

"I am getting ready to pull out now. I have my best friend with me," Gween said.

"OK, we will see you in about an hour," replied Gween.

She hung up and walked over to the bathroom door. Resha came out of the bathroom, smiling.

"So, where are we going?" she asked.

Gween smiled. One thing she could count on was Resha hanging out with her.

"We are going to meet Mr. Married and his friend," replied Gween.

Resha smiled again.

Both ladies looked at themselves in the mirror one last time. They had on black and red Nike dresses with a split by their thighs. Gween's sexy brown tone sparkled in the hotel light. Her brown skin was not a dirty brown, but more of a soft brown. That leg tattoo of a star with money signs all around it on her thigh was as sexy as she was. Her double DD tits sat upright in her push-up bra. Gween was sexy at its finest. Resha was a red bone chick, the size of Kelly Rowland, with J-Lo's ass. Resha had no tattoos, but her bright red skin could light up any room. Along with her all-natural, light blue eyes, these ladies were simply beautiful.

They grabbed their purse and were out of room 226 at Motel Six in the blink of an eye.

NINE

It was a cool Friday night in Savannah, Georgia, with the wind blowing and the air stale. Otis had already checked into his room and called Timothy to see where they were going to hang out. Otis was now standing in his hotel room looking at himself in the mirrors that were in the ceiling. One thing he loved about the Hilton was they had mirrors in the ceiling, which made it easy for you to look at yourself in a different position.

Otis's cell phone rang. He walked over to the TV stand, retrieved his phone, and pushed the speaker button.

"What's up?" a male voice said.

"Nothing, about to make my way to Jay's Seafood and wait on Gween and her girl," Otis replied. Otis then smiled and grabbed his room key from the stand and made his way out the door.

"Nigga, I am already at Jays, so tell me more about Shawty's friend. How does she look?" his friend asked.

Otis started laughing as he closed his room door, then he made his way to the elevator and pushed the down button.

"I have never met her friend, but when I tell you Gween is the shit, my nigga, I know her friend is too," Otis said.

The elevator made a noise and the doors opened. He got inside and pushed L for the lobby.

"You know Tim don't do skinny hoes, and they have to suck dick," joked Tim.

Otis quickly took his friend off the speakerphone. He walked off the elevator and greeted the door attendant.

"Can I get my car? Room 189P," Otis said.

The man looked at a book in front of him and nodded.

"I will be right back with your car," the valet attendant said.

"Yo, you a damn fool. You are very crazy," Otis said playfully.

He looked left and then right.

"OK, let Shawty not suck dick and watch how fast your friend get mad at you," Tim joked.

Otis loved his childhood friend Tim. They lived right next door to each other, went to the same school, same daycare—they did everything together until high school. When they got to high school, Tim's parents got a divorce and moved to Tampa. Even though Tim moved away, he stayed connected with Otis. Whether it was Myspace or Yahoo, they always talked.

"Man, I am waiting for you at Jay's, so bring that ass," Tim said.

Otis laughed and then ended his call.

A few seconds later, the valet attendant came up front with Otis's car. He waited for the guy to come to a stop and opened the front door.

Otis got in his car and sat there for a second. His mind went to thinking about Gween and if she was single. He grabbed the steering wheel and looked out in his rearview mirror. Otis put his car in drive, then made his way into the busy streets of Savannah, GA.

***

"Mama, are you sure you are about to land?" Gail asked.

Gail was tired of sleeping alone and wanted her husband back. She thought of a plan to help her marriage. With her mom being there right before the baby, which would be a tremendous help for her and Otis.

"Yes, Gaily," replied her mom.

Gail was already at Jacksonville International Airport, posted up, waiting for her mom. Gail had not seen her mom since Thanksgiving and really wanted her nearby. She missed her mom so much, and who could she trust more with what she was dealing with?

"I am already here at the airport, waiting for you. You will see me as soon as you exit the plane. You cannot miss me!" replied Gail.

Gail hung up her phone and leaned back in the hard, airport chair. It was uncomfortable and she was starting to hurt. Gail looked at her phone to check to see if Otis had called or texted.

She rushed out of the nail salon, and when she got home, he was already gone. Tim was in town so that meant, once again, what she had planned did not happen. Gail had paid three hundred dollars just to stay at home alone.

"Chicago's plane is now landing," a stewardess said.

Gail got up out of the hard, yellow chair and grabbed her bag from beside her.

"You see that lady? Damn, she is about to burst!" a lady said aloud.

Gail did not even move her head toward the lady.

She knew her belly was poking out. She knew she looked like a blue whale, and she hated that. This pregnancy had taken her body to the max, especially her weight. Gail had gone from a size twelve to a size twenty-two. She had roles in places she never had before. This made Otis not want to touch her or even cuddle with her. This hurt her deeply.

Gail walked over to where they were exiting the plane and waited for her mom. About eight people walked out first before her mom emerged.

"Mommy!" yelled Gail.

Her face lit up like a child in a candy store. She was so excited to see her mom, she did not know what to do with herself. She rushed over to her mom and gave her the biggest, tightest hug ever.

"I miss you, Mom," Gail said.

"Aw, Gaily, you know when you called me crying, I had to stop what I was doing and come straight to your side. You are still my baby girl," Mom said.

They walked over to claim her mother's bags, and then they made their way to the car.

Once they exited the airport, Gail had to stop and sit. The walk just to exit the airport really worked Gail. She was tired and in pain. She rubbed her belly as she closed her eyes.

"How many weeks do you have left? It looks like you are about to have that baby right now," her mom said.

Gail was in so much pain, she did not even reply to her mom. Instead, she rubbed her belly and took deep breaths in and out of her nose. Her mom stood there, watching her take deep breaths. After five minutes of breathing, Gail got up and made her way to the car. Lucky for her, she parked in the handicap spot up front just to make sure she was OK. She even told the men up front where she parked and why.

After walking for about fifteen minutes total, they finally made it to her car. Gail popped the trunk so her mom could toss in her bag.

"Just one bag?" asked Gail.

"A lady always travels light when just visiting," replied her mom.

Gail laughed and flung her head back and looked at the ceiling. That walk put pain on her legs, thighs, and her toes. Suddenly, her whole body started hurting. She felt sharp pains in her stomach and her sides. Gail turned her head toward her mom, then she made an ugly face.

"Are you OK?" her mom asked.

Gail was about to reply, when suddenly, she felt water coming from between her legs.

"Baby, are you pissing on yourself?" joked her mom.

"Now is," said Gail trying to speak.

Gail screamed.

Her mother quickly got on her phone and dialed 911 to get her baby some help. She knew her grandbaby was coming, and boy, was she excited.

"This is Jackie. My daughter is going into labor in the parking garage," yelled Jackie.

TEN

"My name is Timothy, but you can call me Tim. I am Otis's best friend. We have known each other for over ten years and counting," Tim said .

Both ladies looked at him and gave him a fake smile.

"Please tell me he told you lovely ladies about me?" asked Tim.

Otis gave Tim a playful jab to his right arm.

Otis and Tim were now at Jay's Bar and Grill, standing at his table. For this joint to be a brand-new chill spot, it sure looked like it had been open for quite some time now. The place was jammed with so many people. It was packed as if Boosie was in the place. The ladies loved seeing the crowd of people. The view of crowed club with people dancing and having a great time made the ladies smile.. They followed the men to a table in the back of the bar.

Otis had gotten the ladies to come out and have a

drink with them, even though he did not tell them about his boy until the last minute. Tim, on the other hand, was anxious to see what the hype was all about.

For the past month, his best friend had been telling him about a special lady friend. Otis stared at Gween as she made her way to take a seat next to him. He could not get her look out of his mind. He loved the way her curves fit perfectly in the pink Nike dress she was wearing. Her face was so beautiful, her lips favored J-Lo's sexy, thick lips. Otis fell for her looks and her body more than anything.

Otis looked at Gween, and instantly, his mind wandered. He really enjoyed being around her as well as her breathtaking beauty. Her face was not sexy as Gween's, but it was likable. Another thing that turned him away from her was the simple fact that she was a skinny girl. Otis knew his homie loved big girls, and not the small chicken backs.

"I am sorry, but who is your friend?" asked Gween, staring at Tim.

Gween smiled.

She admired her king closely and boy did she love seeing his muscular frame in those buttons up shirts. There was something about Otis that naturally made him extremely sexy to her.

Gween nudged her friend, who was now looking at Tim from head to toe. Tim had on an all-white Nike jogger set with all-white and gray Jordan high top. His arms were not like Otis's, but he was a little buff. Then she recognized he had something shiny hanging out of his ears. He had a big nugget in his ear, along with the ice on his arms. Tim was a flashy person from what she saw and that was not her type.

"Hey there, Tim, I am Gween, and this chick on my side is my best friend, Resha. We are pleased to be here with you two tonight. I hope you can handle the excitement!" Gween said playfully.

Resha then looked at Tim, rolled her tongue over her bottom lip, then smiled. She turned around and put her eyes on Otis. She saw why Gween kept this one on the hush; he was sexy as fuck. His body was more than ten plus, and his arms were a whole different story. Down to the golds in his mouth, he was a ten all across the board.

The ladies sat down at the table, while Tim excused himself to go to the bathroom.

"I will be all right. Let me go pay this water bill," uttered Tim.

Otis laughed, then put his arm around Gween's shoulders. He was beyond happy to see her and wanted to kiss her, but instead, he gave her a hug.

Resha looked at Otis, then to Gween. She saw the shining light in her friend's face. Her whole face was lit up, and she saw it. For once, her bestie was happy. Even if he was not her man, he was for tonight.

"Resha, are you from Brunswick?" Otis asked.

Resha shook her head so fast, it looked like it was going to fall off her neck. She hated Brunswick with a passion till it hit right in the bottom of her stomach. It was not the town itself, but mainly the people who lived in the town. Otis had gotten away to McIntosh, which was not that far from Brunswick, and had pretty much the same people.

"I am from Brunswick, but I do not claim that town," huffed Resha.

Otis looked at her and lowered his head. He was from Brunswick, Georgia, and he understood where she was coming from. That was home, regardless of how the town was.

"I understand what you are saying. Sometimes my town can be sour, but it's home," responded Otis.

Both ladies laughed.

Otis saw Tim coming toward their table with a weird look on his face.

Tim was coming up to the table when he noticed everyone was smiling. He zoned the table, then looked at Otis.

"What did I miss? Why everyone smiling?" Tim asked as he walked up.

Both ladies turned and looked at Tim.

"Nothing happened, we just enjoying our time with you sexy boys," spoke Resha.

"Um... I am not a boy. I am a grown man!" joked Tim.

Everyone laughed.

"Chill out, fam, they just joking with you. That is it!" Otis joked.

The ladies turned their heads and looked at the bar, then back at Otis. He saw their movements and knew they were ready to drink.

"Tim, let's go to the bar and grab these ladies a drink or two," suggested Otis.

Tim looked at Otis and then back at the ladies.

"I mean, only if they want to take a drink from a little boy," Tim snarled.

Gween looked at Otis and rolled her eyes. Otis slowly pushed Tim toward the bar and playfully punched him in the back.

As soon as the men were at the bar, the ladies slid their chairs close to each other.

"Do you think his homeboy is a creep?" Resha asked.

Gween smiled. She knew her bestie was going to ask her about his friend. He did give off an uptight attitude. Gween understood what Resha was saying about his character. Just his vibe that he gave off was weird, simply because of the boy's remark.

Why would he think we called him a little boy?

"It is only one thing you can do about that. You know how we break dudes like that," whispered Gween.

Suddenly, Gween's mouth filled with water. Her stomach twisted in knots, and she slowly put her head down on the table. She grabbed her stomach and looked at Resha, then she jumped up from the table and rushed in the direction of the ladies's room. Resha jumped up behind her and followed her down the blue hallway to the restroom.

Otis turned around and saw the ladies rushing down the hallway. He waited to see if the ladies were going to run out on him. He saw them make a dash for the bathroom, which made him feel a lot better. The last thing he wanted was for them to leave and not even say why.

Otis tugged Tim's arm and then they headed to the

table to wait on the ladies.

"Where did they go?" asked Tim.

Otis shook his head and then pulled out his cell phone. He was just about to send Gween a text when he saw an unfamiliar number. He blinked and rubbed his head.

Why would Gail's mom be calling him? Thanksgiving was the last they saw and spoke to the old hag, thought Otis.

He let the voicemail answer the call instead of him. He was not dealing with her mouth today.

"Damn man, did you cover your ass with your wife? Was that her calling?" Tim asked.

Otis shook his head, then he looked down the hall to see if the ladies were coming back. He stared for about a minute, and still no Gween.

"Nigga, my fat ass wife is OK. She is trying to spend all her time with me," uttered Otis.

"And what the fuck is wrong with that? Nigga, you should have pulled out and then she would not be fat," joked Tim.

Tim started laughing.

Otis did not find him to be funny.

ELEVEN

"Baby, are you OK?" asked Jackie.

Gail blinked and realized she was in the hospital, lying down in the bed. She was in pain and her eyes hurt from the hospital lights shining down on her pupils. She did not even remember coming out of the ambulance and being escorted to the ER at all. The pain had her down so bad, it felt like her whole vagina was about to fall out. The pain was unbelievable and unbearable. She was not feeling this pregnancy and wanted it to be over with.

Gail turned her head and looked to the left side, and there was her mom with a worried look on her face.

Gail reached out for her mom's hand; she took a hold of her arms.

"Did you call Otis?" Gail asked.

Her mom gave her an evil glare and then she shook her head. She did not want to have to break the shocking news to Gail. Bottom line, she called Otis over a dozen times, and she was sent to voicemail.

"Mrs. Gail, how are you doing today?" asked the doctor, coming into the room.

Gail turned and looked toward the door. She saw a pale-skinned man coming inside her room.

"Doctor, have you gotten in touch with my primary doctor, Mr. Stick?" Gail said.

"Honey, I must say, you are far from home, and I doubt your regular doctor will come all the way to Jacksonville, Florida, to deliver a baby," replied the masked doctor.

Gail cried, then she turned to her mother. She wanted her mom to kick this doctor out of the room. There was no way she was going to let another doctor touch her. He did not know her health issues.

"Can I be airlifted home? My husband is going to be very mad that he could not make it," Gail hissed.

The doctor turned and looked at Gail promptly. He did not want to be the bearer of shocking news, but there was no way her doctor was coming down today. Suddenly, that pain that nearly took her off her feet in the parking garage came back ten times as bad as before.

"OH MY FUCKING GOD!" Gail yelled as she grabbed her belly.

The doctor raced over to the monitors that Gail was

hooked up to and read the script that came out. He then went to the front door and yelled, "I need a sonagram done, stat!"

Gail and her mom both had worried looks on their faces. Gail did not understand why she was having all this pain. Never had she been through this with any of her other kids. This had by far been the hardest nine months.

"Can you tell me what is going on? I am having all this pain, sir. I never had this kind of pain before," questioned Gail.

Her mother walked next to her and rubbed her forehead. She saw all the pain and sweat that was being expressed all over her face. Her mother hated that she could do nothing to help her daughter. All she wanted to do was take away all the pain her daughter was having. There was nothing she could do to help Gail ease the pain, and this bothered her down to her toes.

Suddenly, the room door opened, and a group of medical staff rushed in. Each one of the medical team rushed over to Gail.

"Mommy, please try to contact Otis for me. I would love for him to be here. Please keep calling him," whined Gail.

Jackie hated Otis and did not want to call him for

her daughter. She knew right now was not the time to express this to her, so instead, she excused herself and went outside the room. Jackie did not like Otis. She hated his guts. The way he treated her daughter was unacceptable and she wanted Gail to leave his ass.

Jackie called Otis, and despite how she felt about her son-in-law, she let the phone ring until it went straight to voice mail. She made a face. She hated when she was put in a position to have to be the bad guy.

"It's Jackie. Your wife was grabbing me from the airport and her water broke. Please get to St. Joseph Hospital ASAP," Jackie said on his voicemail.

She ended the call, then sent him a text message as well.

Hey Otis, we are at the hospital. Gail has gone in labor, please get to St. Joseph in Jacksonville as soon as you can.

Jackie sent the message, then put her phone in her pocket. She took a deep breath, then she let it out. She knew her daughter was going to overreact once she told her she got no response from Otis. Jackie just shook her head once more and walked back to her daughter's room.

Suddenly, everybody who was in Gail's room was now racing toward Jackie. Jackie was about to run inside the room when she realized they were pushing her daughter. She was shocked.

"What is going on? Where are you taking my child?" shouted Jackie.

"Ma'am, we just got her charts from Savannah and this baby has some kind of heart issue. We must get her prepped for a C-section," the doctor said.

"I am not understanding what you are saying. My daughter has never had to be cut. What is going on?" asked Jackie.

Before she could get a reply, her phone rang. She ignored the phone and watched as they moved her daughter. They hurried and wheeled her to the OR to get her ready for the emergency C-section. Jackie watched as they pushed her daughter down the hallway.

Jackie looked down at her phone, and there was still nothing from Otis. Jackie wondered what was keeping Otis from answering his phone. He was not at work, or was he at home? Jackie quickly called her husband, Josh.

"Hey, baby. Your grand is about to enter the world, and that sorry ass daddy is nowhere to be found," spoke Jackie.

"Honey, why are you in people's business? Did Gail tell you to wonder what is going on?" asked Josh.

Jackie frowned. She knew her husband knew she was up to no good, and she knew he was going to give get in her ass about being in their daughter's love life.

"I have been calling and I sent him a text and still have not heard from him. Plus, they are giving Gail a C-section," Jackie blurted.

"Excuse me? Say what? What is going on with my daughter?" yelled Josh.

Jackie could tell now that she had her husband's attention.

"I do not know what is going on. All I know is they are giving our baby an emergency C-section. I pray someone will tell me something," replied Jackie.

Jackie hung up and took a seat in the front lobby. Now it was just a waiting game. Waiting for Otis to call back, and waiting to see what was going on with her baby. Jackie hated not being back there with her baby girl. She wanted to hold her hands and let her know everything was going to be OK.

Jackie laid her head back against the wall, took a deep breath, then exhaled. Her stomach was in all sorts of knots from her worrying about her daughter.

Ring!

Finally, her phone rang. She looked down at her

caller ID.

She quickly picked up the phone.

"You need to get to St. Joseph Hospital. Your wife is having complications with the baby. They pulled her to the back," Jackie explained.

"Say what? The baby is not due for another three weeks. Did she get you to lie to me?" asked Otis.

Jackie could not believe what had just come from his mouth. Instead of getting upset, she hung up. She refused to sit and fuss with him about his wife.

"Mrs. Jackie, the doctor said you can come back now," a nurse said, approaching Jackie.

Jackie got up from the hard, blue chair and headed toward the nurse. The last thing she was going to do was get out of character with Otis when her baby girl needed her.

TWELVE

"What the fuck is wrong with you? Are you OK?"
Resha asked her friend.

Gween was bent down over the red toilet stool
inside the ladies's bathroom, vomiting her life away. Every
five seconds she was gagging. Her head pounded from all
the gagging she was doing and her nicely slayed install was
everywhere now. The blonde curls were wet and saggy
from her sweating. Suddenly, her stomach started hurting
worse than ever. The pain felt like someone was stabbing
her with a fork. This pain was so unnerving, she held her
stomach tight, but the tighter she held her stomach, the
harder the pain hit.

"I do not know what is going on. I was OK for one
minute, then suddenly, I got sick. My mouth filled with
water, then it was to where I could not control anything.
This pain is sharp and it's shooting down to my pussy,"
Gween said.

Resha looked down at her friend and she looked

terrible. Her wig was all messed up and the color was not popping anymore. She had vomit on her bottom lip, and her shirt was full of it as well. She did not know how to tell her best friend, but with the signs she was looking at, her best friend was pregnant.

"Best friend, are you OK? I do not think you are OK. You really need to get to a Doctor ASAP," stated Resha.

"Look, just go let him know I do not feel so good, and we will hook up another day, please. I am OK, trust me. It may be the seafood we ate earlier."

Resha looked at her friend one last time, then turned around and headed out the door. She hated to burst her best friend's bubble, but she was pregnant. All the signs were there, and she should see that. Suddenly, she was vomiting, head hurting and she could not hold down any food.

I know she is pregnant!

Resha exited the smelly bathroom. It reeked of piss and cigarettes, yet the outside looked like an upscale bar. The only pleasant thing about the bathroom was it had a sitting area in it. Besides that, the bathroom was a total letdown. It had no color to it, just a plain white and gold bathroom with a big screen TV in the sitting area.

Why would you need a seating area in the bathroom?

The way the owner had all the neon lights going on outside, you would think it was DJ Khaled's club. The outside of the bar was lit! The outside had valet parking, as well as a drive-up food truck; it was your neighborhood club in an upscale building.

Resha noticed the hallway had a foul smell as she walked back to their table. The hallway had bloodstains on it as well and some kind of odor she could not identify. Resha wondered why she did not smell this when she was running behind Gween. The smell didn't hit her on the way back. She did not smell any of what she was smelling now.

Resha went and stood next to Tim, who was standing up at the table. They looked like they had just gotten back to the table themselves.

"Hey, Otis, my friend is not feeling well. She wants to know if she can take a rain check?" Resha asked.

Otis looked at her, reached for his cell phone and saw a missed text and call.

Otis got up from the table, then turned and looked at Resha.

"That is OK, I understand. I noticed she was not feeling well so we can take a rain check. I will call her later," Otis replied as he rushed past Resha.

Resha looked at Tim, who was now walking behind Otis. Neither of them was even concerned about what was wrong with her best friend. That was a bummer. Gween was lying around with this nigga and he didn't care.

Suddenly, Tim stopped and walked back over to Resha.

"Can I have your number? After your friend starts feeling a little better, we can spend time together," questioned Tim.

Resha gave him a fake smile. The last thing she wanted was to be with a flashy nigga. The only thing he could do for her was eat her pussy and supply her with cash.

"That is OK with me," she lied.

Tim pulled out his cell phone and placed it in Resha's hand. She took the phone and input her number. She knew he was going to call it, so there was no use in giving him the wrong number. She was stuck with this lame ass nigga.

Tim retrieved his phone and headed the way Otis went. Resha turned and was about to make her way back to her bestie but was stopped when Gween met her halfway down the hall.

"Are you OK?" asked Resha when she saw her bestie.

Gween shook her head, rubbed her face, then made her way back to the table they were sitting at. As Gween got closer to the table, she saw the guys were gone.

"What happened?" asked Gween.

Resha shook her head, confused.

"You told me to tell them we were going in because you're sick," answered Resha.

Gween shook her head. She looked toward the door, then back at her friend.

"What are we going to do? I am feeling a lot better," asked Gween.

Resha was not worried about what they were doing; her main concern was what was going on with her best friend. The signs she was giving off were not sitting right with Resha. Something was up with her friend, and she wanted to get to the bottom of it.

"Look, bitch, we are going to grab a pregnancy test, and then you are going to take that bitch,' explained Resha.

Gween looked at her friend with her mouth wide open, not feeling it. The last thing she wanted was a baby right now. She had so much going on right now and was not ready for a baby. Plus, Otis was married.

"I understand you care for me, but bitch, there is no baby in my stomach. I am just sick because of the food I ate earlier. You know I cannot eat seafood and I ate some. Come on, why are you putting bad luck on my name?" huffed Gween.

Resha was not buying the small talk; she knew something what was up. Plus, her bestie was acting shitty. She was not acting herself and was always sick. She knew all too well what was going on, Gween was just in disbelief.

"When are you going to the doctor?" asked Resha.

Gween looked at her homie and rolled her eyes. She was not for this today, and she could tell Resha was not going to let this end.

"Let's roll up to the Dollar Tree we drove past on the way here," suggested Resha.

"Man, see, now you are tripping!" Gween yelled.

Both ladies got up and made their way out toward the exit. Luckily, the ladies drove themselves to the bar, because from the look of it, the fellas were gone.

Gween made her way to her car, which was parked at the end closer to the road. The ladies were now at the intersection of MLK and High Points. Gween pushed the button on her phone to alert the alarm. She knew they'd parked in the back, but now that the whole parking lot was full, it was hard for her to find her car.

BEEP! BEEP!

The ladies heard the alarm and looked in the direction from which it was coming. They slowly walked over to Gween's car. There was a group of men standing close by her car who caught the ladies's attention. They looked up and saw the group of sexy men standing, pouring out some liquor. Resha was already speaking before Gween could get a full view of the eye candy.

"Excuse me, fellas!" snapped Resha.

The group of men turned around and looked at them.

"I'm saying, what is good with you two sexy ladies?" the red boy asked.

Gween's eyes examined the whole group. She did not want to talk to anybody now. She was in so much pain, all she wanted to do was lay down.

"I am straight. You have a great night," Gween replied.

The group of men sucked their teeth, then turned around and walked off. Resha smiled to herself. For some reason, she found this to be funny to her.

The ladies got into Gween's car; Resha was driving.

She did not want her best friend to try to drive with the pain she was having.

The ladies turned out of the packed parking lot. Resha looked around one more time before she pulled out. The parking lot was thick, thicker than the inside. There were so many dudes outside with their music up loud, coolers with beer and liquor and ladies twerking. Outside was where the party was at, from the looks of it.

Honk!

Resha jumped. She had been at the stop sign for about ten minutes, examining the parking lot. The line of cars behind her now had appeared out of nowhere. She peeked at her rearview mirror, then exited the parking lot.

Resha looked over to her best friend. Her skin was not glowing; she looked sick. Gween held her stomach to try to control the pain. Resha hated it when her bestie was down, and there was nothing she could do to fix the issue.

"Where are we going?" Gween said.

Resha turned to the Abercorn Connections and got in the far-right lane. She turned around and looked at her friend.

"You need to see a doctor. We are going to the ER," answered Resha.

Gween grunted, but she knew there was no way she

could change her best friend's mind. Once her mind was made up, there was no way to stop her. She was like a shark, scoping out its prey. She knew the best thing for her to do was just be quiet and let Resha do what she wanted.

THIRTEEN

Gail blinked, took a deep breath, then exhaled. Suddenly, she felt a sharp pain in her side. She flinched just a little. She tried to move her leg, then noticed there was something tied to her legs. She blinked again, then looked down at her feet. They were so swollen; she could not see her toes. Then she noticed two white bags tied to her ankles. She turned her head and looked toward the window and noticed it was night. The room was a peachy yellow color, with baby blue ducks on the walls. A TV was on the wall in front of her, a baby blue and white crib was hooked up right next to her bedside, along with her IV machine.

Gail took a deep breath. Suddenly, her stomach started hurting. She tried to cough, and it nearly killed her. Her insides ached; her stomach hurt even worse when she tried to move.

Gail blinked.

"Are you awake?" someone asked.

Gail looked up and saw Otis standing at the foot of

her bed. She was just looking there and had not seen Otis. She smiled so hard, she forgot the reason she was even in pain.

Gail tried to sit up, but she had no luck. Gail's right arm had an IV in it, and a blood pressure cuff hooked up to her. Her left arm had another puncture site with white sterile tape on it. This made trying to get up extremely complicated. All she wanted to do was get up and hug her husband.

Gail made an unpleasant look. She wanted to get up and hug her husband, but right now, her body had another plan and that did not include her body moving.

"When did you get here? What took you so long?" asked Gail.

She looked at Otis's clothing and realized he was dressed to go out. He had on his good clothes.

"Does it matter? I am here now, right? Besides, why are you trying to move?" answered Otis.

Gail rolled her eyes. As bad as she missed her husband, he could miss her with the smart-ass comments. Besides, her body felt like she had been jumped by ten girls. Gail jerked her arm when the blood pressure cuff started rising.

"Why must you come in here with all that? I just

asked when you came in," hollered Gail.

Otis looked at Gail. By the look on his face, Gail could tell she had finally gotten his attention.

"What is your problem? Who do you think you are yelling at? I can march my ass straight out this hospital!" snapped Otis.

Before he got a reply, Jackie emerged from the bathroom.

"Why are you guys yelling? What is wrong with you? Gail just had a baby for Jesus's sakes," whispered Jackie.

Jackie walked toward Gail's door, peeped out the door, then closed it. She then turned around and walked over to Gail's bed and took a seat at the foot. She looked at Otis, shook her head and laid her eyes on Gail. She was beyond embarrassed by how both were yelling and carrying on. She was in total shock.

"Mom, I just asked a question, and it was like I was out of line for asking," Gail murmured.

Otis gave his wife the most gruesome look. Gail knew she had made Otis mad, but she did not care.

"Have you met your son? Have you been to the nursery?" Jackie asked.

Otis hated it when Jackie was around because all

she did was take Gail's side on everything. He felt Jackie was the reason Gail's attitude changed.

One day, he woke up and she was acting like her mom, even down to her body shape.

"No, I have not. I came straight to Gail to make sure she was OK. The doctor told me she had a C-section, and it put a strain on her heart," Otis replied.

Gail's mouth slid open. She was shocked he took a phone call from the doctor because she sure could not get him to pick up her phone calls.

"Carlton Anthony is his name. He weighs nine pounds, sixteen ounces and seventeen inches long," Jackie stated.

Otis's whole face lit up like a firecracker. None of his other sons were born that juicy. He was ready to see him now. Otis walked toward the room door, turned, and looked at Gail.

"I am going to see Carlton, if that is OK with you?" snickered Otis.

Gail did not answer that dumb ass question. Instead, she turned and looked at her mom. Otis exited the door and left the two ladies alone to gossip about him, something they did all the time.

"Baby, now I was married to your father for over

thirty years, and I know when a man is cheating. That man is cheating. I smelled a woman's perfume on him," Jackie explained.

Gail did not want to hear that; she was happy he was here.

"Mom, really?" questioned Gail.

"I am only telling you what I know," answered Jackie.

Both ladies jumped at a loud noise.

They looked over toward the sink and saw what was making the noise. It was Otis's phone vibrating on the sink. Jackie jumped up off the foot of the bed and walked toward the phone.

"Mom, don't!" yelled Gail.

Jackie ignored her daughter and reached for Otis's phone. She pulled her glasses down over her eyes and looked at his phone.

"Mom!" blurted Gail.

Jackie raised her eyes and put them right back in the phone.

"Well, at least let me see!" begged Gail.

Her mom slowly walked over and took a seat at the foot of the bed.

"I knew it!" yelled Jackie.

Gail's heart skipped a beat, and she almost pooped in her bed when she heard her mom yell.

"Mom, please do not do that. I just had a baby," Gail joked.

"Baby, he is cheating on you. There is a text from some woman that says she enjoyed their time together," babbled Jackie.

Gail's eyes filled with tears, and there was a pain in her head and side now. Gail reached for her husband's phone and looked through it.

"Do not get mad. You are my child and stuff like this, we do not let the other woman win. Honey, you are going to fight for your husband," Jackie said.

Gail did not hear anything she was saying. Her eyes were glued to the messages she was reading.

"Gail!" Jackie yelled.

Gail lifted her head slowly, then she looked at her mama.

"I am fine, trust me. That message is a mistake," Gail huffed.

Jackie glanced at her daughter and then back at the room door. She saw the pain in her daughter's eyes, but she also saw something that made her terribly upset. She saw how stupid her daughter was. Even with cold, hard proof, she still was in denial.

"Can you please put the phone back on the sink?" Gail demanded.

Jackie reached for the phone, but Gail jerked it back.

Jackie was about to say something when her daughter spoke.

"Wait a second, let me screenshot this message and number," Gail uttered.

Jackie watched as her daughter tried to slide up in the bed, but she failed. Jackie got up off the foot of the bed, reached over to the nightstand, and grabbed Gail's phone. She snapped a picture and quickly walked back over to the sink and placed the phone back to how she found it lying.

Gail was about to say something when the doctor knocked on her door.

"Hello, Dr. Smith," a man said from behind her door.

Jackie rushed over to the door to open it. The doctor and a nurse walk inside with paperwork. Gail looked at their faces, then at her mom. She was afraid of what was going to happen. From their looks, neither the doctor nor nurse came to play. Neither of them was smiling. She took a deep breath and braced herself for what was going to be

I ' M HAVING HIS BABY TOO

said.

FOURTEEN

"Are you OK?" questioned Resha.

Gween was lying down in the Memorial Hospital ER department. Somehow, she had gotten talked into coming to get checked. They took a urine sample, blood count and nose swab. Now it was a waiting game, and it was driving Gween crazy. In the midst of her waiting for results, she suddenly started feeling better and wanted to leave now. Resha was not going for that shit, however. Gween was going to make her ass wait on these results today.

"What is going on with you? You see, I feel so much better. Resh, let's get the fuck out of here."

Resha looked up out of her phone and then back down. She was not trying to hear anything her best friend had to say. Right now, all that matters is what these results say. If she had to nail her ass down in the bed, they were getting these results today.

Gween leaned up in the hospital bed and slid her

legs over the bed to dangle. She was ready to go. She hated waiting for something, and she especially hated hospitals. Ever since she lost her father in the hospital, she did not feel they were safe.

"Where are you going? Your doctor has not come in with any results. Explain to me where you are going," pouted Resha.

Gween heard her tone and immediately knew she was dead serious. This was not her just playing with Gween; she meant what she said and stood strong on her decision.

"OK, you do not have to be so fucking rude," answered Gween.

Resha sucked her teeth and rolled her eyes. She did not care how much Gween looked mad; she was waiting for these results today.

Gween jumped off the bed and reached for her clothes on the sink. She was about to put on her pants when there was a knock at the door.

"Yes!" answered Resha.

Gween jumped and raced to the bathroom, slamming the door behind her.

"Hello, I am P.A. Jones. Where is the lucky

patient?" asked the doctor.

"She just raced to the bathroom, she will be out shortly," replied Resha.

Gween emerged out of the bathroom and took a seat back on the bed.

"Yes, doctor," Gween mumbled.

"Aw, don't sound so down," Dr. Jones answered.

"Can you tell me what is going on? What is causing me to be OK one minute and sick the next?" Gween asked.

Dr. Jones looked in the papers he brought with him into the room.

"I will begin with your hormone levels. T are so high, you are dehydrated, and you have a UTI," he said.

Gween looked at Resha, then went back to the doctor.

"I am OK then, right?" Gween mumbled.

"Yes, you are fine, but I suggest you get on some fluids for the baby's sake," answered Jones.

Gween's legs became very numb, and she had to lean back on the bed. Her ears itched, and her eyes hurt. Suddenly, her body felt light, so she leaned back a little more on the bed.

"Baby?" Resha asked.

"Yes, ma'am. From the blood work, you are about

six weeks. Happy Valentine's Day," Dr. Jones said.

Gween went from leaning against the bed, to falling to the floor.

Gween lost control of her legs, and they gave out on her. Resha jumped up and rushed over to her bestie on the floor.

"Are you OK? Do not move her," demanded Jones.

Jones went down to the floor and started rubbing Gween's stomach and legs.

"I am OK. My head started hurting. But did you say pregnant?" Gween asked.

Dr. Jones laughed. He knew she was in a state of shock and just wanted to make sure she was OK.

"Yes, you are pregnant. Now do not frighten me like that. You are falling will not look good on my resume. Please get up off the floor," pleaded Dr. Jones.

Resha and Jones helped Gween off the floor and up on the bed. She sat back and stared off into space. She looked right at the doctor and Resha, but her mind looked past them.

Jones waved his hands in front of Gween's face but got no reaction. He was worried now. He was about to step closer, then Resha held up one finger. He took a step back and let Resha take a seat next to her best friend.

"Baby Girl, are you OK?" Resha asked.

Gween was still shocked by what the doctor had just told her. How could she be pregnant when she was on the pill? She had not missed a pill doasage. What was really going on?

"Doctor, are you serious?" Gween finally asked.

Jones looked at Gween and smiled. He thought the situation was something lovely and not bad. He had no idea how much this would set Gween back.

"I am OK, trust that," Gween mumbled

Dr. Jones looked at Gween and then back at Resha.

"Well, we are going to discharge you in just a second. Let me sign off on your paperwork and then you are free to leave," Dr. Jones said as he exited the room.

Resha looked at Gween, smiled, then folded her arms across her chest. Gween looked at her best friend and knew what was coming up next.

Here it was, two days before Valentines Day, and she was pregnant. What in the world did God have in store for her? It must not be good.

"Are you going to tell him?" Resha mumbled.

Gween acted like she did not hear her. She kept tying her Air Forces and ignored Resha's question.

Resha cleared her throat, then she got up off the

foot of the bed and grabbed Gween's hand.

"Baby, did you hear me?" she asked.

Gween had no choice but to stop what she was doing and listen to her. She had her attention and her arm. Resha was serious, this time.

"I heard you, loud and clear, trust me," answered Gween.

When it comes to kids, Resha was serious because she was raped when she was eight and it ruined her. Now she could not have any kids. So when the issue of kids came up, she took it very seriously.

"You know that man is married and lives with his wife," Gween said.

With that reply, Resha said nothing. Instead, she went and took a seat on the visitor chair and just stared at her friend.

Both ladies waited in silence, staring at the next. There were more questions that needed to be answered.

Gween was not up for the twenty-one questions; she was ready to get back to the room and head back to Brunswick, Georgia.

****

Otis glanced through the window to try to find his baby. He stood there for about five minutes, then patted his back pocket.

"Fuck," he spoke.

He had left his phone on the sink in Gail's room. He knew he had fucked up now.

He looked at the row of babies and shook his head. He did not know which one was his baby. He was embarrassed and lowered his head.

"How can I help you?" a woman asked.

Otis picked up his head and looked in the direction of the voice.

"Hello, I am OK," Otis replied.

He looked up and saw the same lady who was standing by the elevator when he got off, had now come over and addressed him.

"My wife is in room two-eleven. She just had our baby boy," Otis bragged.

The nurse smiled.

"I am Nurse Jenny. I am on shift this morning. Do you have a wristband that identifies who you are?" Jenny asked.

Otis knew by her tone that she was not with it. Plus, he did not have a wristband to show who he was and his baby's name.

"I will go and get the information from my wife and

then come back," Otis said.

"You do that, sir. She should have told you that," Jenny informed him.

Otis walked back to the elevator, mad as hell. He had really made a blank trip, could not see his son, and had left his phone.

This day could not get any worse, thought Otis.

FIFTEEN

Otis walked back into his wife's room and saw Jackie with her face twisted up. He took a quick glance at the sink to see if his phone was still in the same spot. He always examined Gail's face to see if there was anything unusual on her face. Her face wasn't screwed up like her mother's, so he assumed she wasn't mad.

"Did you see Carlton? How was he?" Jackie asked.

Otis politely ignored her and walked over to the sink, retrieved his phone, and stood at the foot of Gail's bed. He looked at his wife and saw she had been crying. Her face was red and swollen. Her eyes were puffier than ever, and it looked like she hadn't gotten a wink of sleep in the last twenty-four hours.

"Are you OK? When did they say you can go home?" Otis asked.

Jackie stood beside Otis and looked at her daughter.

"I am going home in two days. They are running

some tests on me and the baby to make sure he is OK and healthy to go home," answered Gail.

Otis replaced Jackie in the chair she had been in, then he pulled out his phone.

"I need a wristband to see the baby. They did not let me see him," blurted Otis.

"When did you plan on telling me you needed a wristband?" scolded Jackie.

Otis was about to say something when he looked at his wife, then she winked for him to let it go.

"I will page the nurse and get you a band," Gail suggested.

She pushed the help button and laid her head back on her pillow. The last thing she wanted was for her mother and husband to fight when she needed them both. *Why did they fuss so much?*

"I am going to step out and return Tony's phone call," Otis explained as he headed to the door.

Gail knew he was lying. She had just examined his phone and David was nowhere in there. There was a missed call from someone who was saved under "Young". Gail knew that was who he was going to call back.

As he stepped out of the room, Gail cried.

"Excuse me, why are you crying? Why are you

letting this shitface do you like this?" questioned Jackie.

Gail paid her mom no attention. Instead, her mind wondered about what her husband was saying to this lady. She wanted to know every detail about her; what she did for a living and how she met Otis.

Gail's thoughts were shattered when the knock came on her door.

"Come in!" yelled Gail.

She was so mad, she did not even realize she yelled at the top of her lungs. Her voice echoed through the room. Jackie's attention was glued on her daughter at this moment.

"What is the matter with you, Gail Anne?" Jackie asked.

Gail did not care what her mom had to say at this point; she was furious and wanted answers.

Before Jackie could ask another question, in walked the nurse with Baby Carlton.

"Hey, Mommy, we just wanted to bring this bundle of cuteness for some snack," the nurse said.

Gail smiled as she saw the blue blanket. She was ready to see her son. She couldn't remember what happened at birth. Gail remembered being told she was given medicine to calm her because her blood pressure was too high.

The nurse walked over to Gail's bed and Gail took a deep breath and reached her arms out. Jackie stood, looking on with the biggest smile ever.

"Mrs. Gail, this here is Carlton," the nurse said as she unwrapped the baby.

Gail's heartbeat extremely fast. She blinked and looked down at her precious baby boy.

Oh my God, he looks like Otis. Damn, he has his dimples and his bushy eyebrows.

Gail looked at her baby and instantly rubbed her nose all over his face. She could not believe how cute and chubby he was. His hair was slicked back on his pretty little head, his fingers were tiny, and his face was round. Gail then lifted his shirt and slowly rubbed his belly. Carlton wiggled.

Jackie chuckled.

Carlton moved his head from side to side, then he cried a little. He rubbed his face on Gail's breast.

"Feeding time," Gail whispered.

"All right, let me leave you two," the nurse said.

Gail pulled out her breast and positioned Carlton to latch on. Gail wiggled her nipple in front of his lips. He opened his mouth and latched on as if he already knew what to do.

Jackie looked at her daughter and smiled. She loved seeing her daughter happy instead of being upset and stressed out. Seeing her with Baby Carlton, it made her forget all about Otis and his bullshit.

Carlton sucked the milk from his mother's breast.

"Mom, this is so precious. I wish Otis could be here," suggested Gail.

Jackie's smile went away. She hated the hell out of Otis.

"Why can't we enjoy a moment without him?" asked Jackie.

Gail paid her mom no attention; her mind and soul were fixed on her son. He was the most precious gift anybody could ask for.

"Mom, Carlton is more than perfect!" Gail said.

Jackie went closer to her daughter and grandson. She stared at them for about thirty seconds, then smiled the biggest smile.

"I have an idea, but I don't know if you are going to like this one," Jackie blurted.

Gail took her eyes off her baby and glanced at her mom. She wondered what idea she had conjured up.

"I am listening," Gail uttered.

Jackie took a deep breath, then she pushed her hair back from out of her face. She wanted Gail to see her face and understand she was trying to help the best she could.

"Baby, having a new baby is a struggle, especially with a cheating husband," Jackie vocalized.

Gail's face went completely sour, turning into a frown.

"We are not going to talk about Carlton's father like that! Come on, Mom!" Gail said angrily.

Jackie knew by mentioning that evil ass name, she was going to get upset. She did not want to upset her daughter, but she wanted to give her some guidance. She did not want her daughter to deal with heart ache while dealing with having a newborn.

"What you are not going to do is yell at me. You are not your father," snapped Jackie.

Gail removed her breast from her son's mouth, then she burped him. She laid him over her shoulder and lightly patted him on the back.

"I am not going back home just yet. I am planning to stay around and help you with the other kids and the baby," mumbled Jackie.

Gail snatched her head and looked at her mom. She did not know whether to be happy or sad about this. She wanted her mom's help, but she did not have the energy to deal with her and Otis taking shots at each other. She just did not. This was something she would have to think hard on and get Otis's opinion on before deciding.

"Mom, let me talk with Otis," Gail said.

"Excuse me? Who is he? He is not my boss or your boss," blurted Jackie.

Gail knew this was not going to end, so it made no sense in going back and forth with Jackie. This was one of those times you let your parents have it.

Knock!

"Yes!" Jackie yelled.

The door opened, and in ran Gail's other four kids.

"Mommy!"

All the boys were excited to see their mom.

Chris, Alphature, Kareem and PJ raced over to their mom's bed. They examined their baby brother.

"Mommy, how did he get here?" PJ asked.

"Mommy, why he has so much hair?" Kareem asked.

Everybody laughed.

Gail then looked at Shelia. She saw she was tired. She had had her kids for over a week now.

"Shelia, I want to say thank you for everything that

you are doing to help me. My mom will be here for I do not know how long, but I can give you a break," explained Gail.

"Grandma staying with us?" her oldest, Chris, asked.

Jackie playfully punched Chris in his side and he fell to the ground.

"Grandma, that is not nice!" joked Chris.

"Do you boys want to get in my bed and see your brother up close?" Gail asked.

Everybody smiled and dashed for her bed.

"Wait, one at a time," demanded Jackie.

Chris went first and crawled up on the bed with his mother. He looked at his baby brother and was filled with smiles. He was overfilled with joy.

"Mommy, can he talk?" asked Chris.

Gail laughed.

"No, baby, he can't talk yet. All he can do right now is cry," joked Gail.

"Mama, you mean all he going to do is cry?" Chris asked, confused.

Before Gail could assure her son that everything was OK, there was a knock on her door again.

PJ dashed for the door but was too late. The nurse

had already opened the door and was now walking inside.

"I see we have the whole family visiting baby brother today!" the nurse said.

Jackie pulled PJ and Kareem back and pushed them in the chair so the nurse could have room to do what she needed to do.

SIXTEEN

"Hey, hello, how are you doing?" whispered Otis.

Otis was on the phone, returning his missed phone call to Gween. He had excused himself from Gail's room and walked down to the waiting area. He wanted to get far away from the door so Gail or her wicked mother could not hear his conversation.

"I'm fine, what about yourself?" Gween asked.

Otis huffed. The way she answered him sounded like she was mad or something. Her tone sent off vibes that something was wrong. He had been talking to her on and off for about a month now, and he knew when something was wrong.

"I had to rush out, she had the baby last night," Otis explained.

Gween looked at her phone.

Who is she? thought Gween.

"Congratulations, I know you are going to be the best dad," Gween said dryly.

Otis thought about what she said. He had not even told her he had other kids, but he had told her he was married.

"Please stop that. It is nothing to be happy about," uttered Otis.

Gween heard and did not hear.

"Look, call me back later. Me and Resha about to hit the highway and head home," Gween said.

"I am happy, OK? I am sorry I did not tell you it was this soon," explained Otis.

Click!

Gween hung up.

Otis looked at his phone, saw it said the call ended, then sucked his teeth. She was pissed and him being here with Gail did not make the situation any better.

"Excuse me!" the nurse said.

Otis turned his head and saw a lady standing in all blue behind him with a chart.

"Yes," replied Otis.

"I was told that you tried to see your son and they denied you," the nurse said.

Otis nodded.

"Well, I just took him in with Mom for feeding time. You can go in if you like," suggested the nurse.

Otis gave her a shy smile and headed down the hallway toward Gail's room. He knew she was watching to make sure that was where he went. He got outside of Gail's room and turned and looked back down the hall at the nurse to see if she was still watching him.

He turned, and there she stood, watching him with her hands folded across her chest. Her face was all screwed up. He wondered what the problem was and why she was acting like he stole something.

Otis entered his wife's room.

"Daddy!" PJ yelled.

Otis was shocked when he saw his other children, especially when he saw Shelia. Shelia was very attractive to him, so he tried his best to stay away from her.

"What is going on, my man?" Otis asked playfully.

Gail glanced up at Otis and smiled.

"Hello, Mr. Otis," Shelia said.

Otis nodded and went and took a seat by the window. PJ, Kareem, Alphature and Chris all dashed over to their father's side, jumping right into his lap, and started playing with their daddy. The boys were too excited to see their father and missed him dearly. It had been over two weeks since they'd last seen their dad, so seeing him now was a burst of excitement.

"Where have you been, Dada?" Kareem asked.

Otis played with his boys, tickling one, while trying to bite the other ones. All of them acted like a bunch of small kids. Otis loved his boys and would not trade them for the world.

Jackie watched Otis closely as he played with her grandchildren. She did not trust that man for shit, and hated him with a passion.

"Gail, when do you think they are going to let you come home?" Shelia asked.

Gail took a deep breath and looked at her mother, who stared at Otis and the kids. Gail wanted to say something, but she did not want to fuss in front of her kids.

"I do not know now. This was my first time having to be cut. I will tell you this, though. I am in so much pain, I can barely bear to hold Carlton on my chest right now," uttered Gail.

Shelia frowned.

"I can take the kids home and get the house all set for you and Carlton," suggested Jackie.

Gail turned her head and looked at her mother.

Now why would she say that? She knows I have not even talked to Otis about her wanting to stay.

"I think that would be nice. At least she will be able

to get some sleep," answered Shelia.

Suddenly, a cold rush of air rushed into the room. It seemed as if everyone felt the wind because everybody stopped talking. The room got quiet and stale; even the boys had stopped playing with their father and were standing, looking at him. Gail felt a gushing wind pass by her face and blinked.

"Why would you want to do all that for Gail when I am here? And Shelia?" Otis asked.

Jackie did not even look at him. Instead, she kept her eyes on Gail.

"I did just ask a fucking question?" blurted Otis.

Jackie turned around this time and looked at him. She looked at him up and down, then sucked her teeth.

"Look, you two, before the yelling starts," Gail said.

"I have the right to know what is going on," Otis demanded.

Otis was beyond furious. He was huffing so hard, they all saw his chest beating through his shirt. He stood there, glancing at Jackie, then Gail.

"Mom is staying with us for a while. You know I just had a C-section so I am going to need more help than before. Besides, you have to work, so yes, she is staying to help me," explained Gail.

120

"Daddy, Grandma staying with us?" Alphature asked.

"Apparently, she is. It seems like Mommy pays all the bills and I do nothing, son, answered Otis.

Alphature looked at his father, confused. He did not understand what he was saying. The only thing that registered in his little mind was yes, his grandma was staying.

Gail glanced at Shelia sharply, Jackie, then her kids.

Otis was rude and disrespectful all the time. He did not care who was around when he opened his mouth.

Otis walked past his kids, then made his way toward the door.

"I will see you when you get home. From the looks of it, you do not need me here," mumbles Otis.

Gail's mouth fell wide open as she watched her husband leave her room. Tears came down her cheeks and she took a deep breath, and slowly exhaled.

Gail was beyond furious. All she wanted to do right now was run behind Otis.

"What else do you need to see? That man is cheating on you!" exclaimed Jackie.

Shelia looked at Gail and shook her head. She had been their babysitter for over five years and all she had seen was Gail cry and beg. She did not understand why she just wouldn't take her kids and walk away. With the drama Otis had put her through, she must be tired.

"Shelia, tell me something. Have you witnessed anything strange with Otis? You are there more than me, so tell me what you have witnessed," Jackie asked.

"Not in front of my kids, please," pleaded Gail.

Jackie looked at Shelia, and something in her gut told her she knew something about Otis.

Jackie rolled her eyes.

"I will take the boys home, so you can get some rest with the new baby," Shelia suggested.

Gail nodded.

"Come give Mommy a kiss," Gail said to her boys.

Jackie took Baby Carlton from Gail and placed him in the crib. The boys all raced over to their mother's bedside.

"I love you guys, and I need you guys to be nice to Ms. Shelia until me and your baby brother come home," Gail said.

All the boys threw up high fives. She dapped them up.

"Mom, are you going with them?" asked Gail.

Jackie did not answer. Instead, she walked over to the recliner, grabbed her bag, and headed toward the door.

"Come on, boys, it's pizza night!" she said excitedly.

SEVENTEEN

"I swear I feel like I am in some type of entanglement," joked Otis.

Otis sat in the break room inside of Publix. He was sitting among three of his coworkers: Jason, Josh, and Avery. These three young men had been working with Publix for over eight years now. Not Otis, but they had put in a lot of work. These three men were the only ones in the store Otis trusted with his personal life. Over the years, they had become extremely close. All of them were married, except Avery. He was the single bachelor of the group. Avery kept a condom in his back pocket for reasons like this.

"Nah, what you have is a case of new pussy, and now, my boy, you are stuck headfirst in the sea," joked Avery.

Everybody laughed.

Otis looked around the break room and shook his head. In the break room was wall to wall reminders about work-related stuff, and other important information pertaining to the job. The walls were painted gray with green stripes, and it had one microwave that barely worked. The floor sparkled like someone had just buffed it, but then there was gum stuck in the corners. This room really needed a makeover. After all these years of working here, none of the associates complained about the break room.

Josh playfully hit Otis on his arm to grab his attention.

"Yo, are you OK?" asked Josh.

"I am going to say it since none of you dicks said it. What in the hell made you step out on Gail?" asked Jason.

The men got quiet and looked at Otis.

"I mean, I cannot answer that, because you already know what happened," replied Otis.

"Just admit it, you wanted your dick sucked, and Gail wasn't sucking that pipe right," Avery joked.

Everyone laughed, except Jason.

Jason turned his head, looked at Avery, and gave him an evil eye..

"Me and Sasha have been married for ten years, and I have never stepped out on her. No matter how mad she gets at me, I am not cheating," blurted Jason.

Avery heard his tone and let it go. He knew Jason

was big on marriage and he was not the one to cheat. But what he was not going to do was ruin this man's day because he got some new pussy. Avery glanced at Jason and smiled. He let him think he had it, but he didn't have shit.

"Let me ask you this, Jason. Have you thought that maybe Gail is not satisfying this man right? I mean, why would someone cheat?" Avery asked.

"Look, I am not about to sit here and let you guys fight and fuss over what I do with my dick?" joked Otis.

"Nigga, I'on care what you do with your dick," Jason answered sharply.

Otis walked over to the purifying water machine, pulled down a cup, then placed it right under the slot. Otis turned around and faced his crew.

"I am OK, I just think about Gween a lot more than I should be," uttered Otis.

"When are you finding time to hang with this Gween, if Gail just had a baby?" Jason asked.

Otis laughed.

Otis grabbed his water cup from under the machine and made his way to the door.

"Well, where is the picture of the baby? You have not said anything about him? Why is that?" questioned

Jason.

"Damn, my guy, you sure that's his baby? You are acting like you the FBI," joked Avery.

The fellas paid him no attention.

"The baby pushed me away. I am tired of every time I turn around, my wife's a fucking whale," revealed Otis.

Josh and Jason were shocked at their friend. They could not believe that their friend was saying these awful things about Gail. Gail had given him five wonderful kids, and he was putting her down like that.

Nobody spoke for a hot minute. Instead, they all just looked at Otis.

"If you feel like that, then why don't you leave?" questioned Jason.

Otis knew he was coming with something behind what he had just said.

"Otis does not have to leave nowhere he isn't ready. He is trying to find out if Gail is what he wants still," commented Avery.

This conversation had gone sour so fast when all he wanted was some advice. Why must they drill him about his wife? Why must they take what he said and turn him into the bad guy? *It never fails. I am always the bad guy.*

"Y'all have been listening to me bitch for years about Gail. I mean, come on, cut me some slack here. I have stuck around for all this time for what? My wife does not excite me anymore," Otis responded.

Everybody stopped what they were doing and looked at Otis. Even Avery was shocked at the words he'd just heard.

"Brother man, just do what makes you happy if you want to leave, then leave. As a man, if you are not happy, then you are right, why are you wasting your time?" Jason asked.

Otis looked at his homies and walked over to the punch out clock.

"Where are you going? You do not get off till six a.m. just like us?" chimed Avery.

Otis smiled and punched out. He walked to the door and put his hand on the knob.

"When you have an ass of PTO, you can leave whenever you want to. Especially when you have a weekend planned," joked Otis.

Before the fellas got a word out, he was outside the door, just like that. It was a gloomy Friday afternoon, and he had plans to spend the weekend with Gween in Jacksonville.

It had been six days since Gail had been home with the baby, and he needed some away time. The crying Carlton was doing was not making the house noise level any less quiet than before. Even though this was his fifth child, it seemed like the level of noise was getting worse.

Otis said goodbye to his colleagues as he walked out of the billion-dollar franchisee. He was about to go through the exit doors when someone caught his eye. He double looked to make sure what he was seeing was correct. There, checking out at customer service, was Resha, looking sexy as fuck. He could not come to grips with how sexy she was, standing in the line. He blinked his eyes, then turned his head and looked to see if he was seeing Gween.

"Hey, Otis," Resha said.

Otis smiled.

Resha retrieved the paper from the clerk and headed over toward Otis at the double doors. She smiled as she got closer.

"Damn, I had no idea you worked here. I come here all the time and shop. This is a small town, I guess," joked Resha.

They walked out of Publix and made their way across the busy parking lot.

"Where is your sidekick?" joked Otis.

Resha walked up to a candy blue Chevy Impala, opened the door, and jumped inside of it. Then she let the window down and stared at Otis.

"It was nice seeing you in those work clothes," giggled Resha.

Otis smiled, then stepped away from her car. He watched her drive out of the parking lot.

Damn, that bitch is fine, he thought.

Then he shook his head.

Otis made his way to his car, parked all the way across the parking lot. Employees could not park in front of the store. They had their own parking lot dedicated to Publix workers.

As he made his way toward his car, his phone chimed. Just by the ring tone, he knew who was calling.

"What?" asked Otis.

"Baby, I know you said you have that big trip out of state with the fellas for work, and I was wondering, um, since my mom is here, can I tag along and bring more support?" Gail asked.

Otis smiled. He loved how she tried to make this all about him and her. He knew she wanted to spy on him. Gail had been acting very weird lately and he just could not understand the change in demeanor. Gail had gone from not cooking to cooking, cleaning up and washing clothes. This was something she had stopped a long time ago. The more kids she had, the lazier and fatter she became. Otis hated that.

"Look, I already told you that you just had Carlton. He is not even two months yet."

"He will be two months in eight more days," answered Gail.

"My point. So, with that, you cannot go with me. I do not trust your mom around my newborn," blurted Otis.

Otis got in his car and cranked it up. He was not about to let his wife ruin the weekend he had planned. After all the crying that had been going on in the house, he at least needed some type of free time.

Otis hung up in his wife's face and had no remorse. It was his weekend, and he was going to enjoy every bit of it.

EIGHTEEN

Gween stood up and looked at herself in the hotel mirror that was on the decked-out white and gold wall. The gold strip was so bright and shiny, she loved it. She could not believe she was going to be someone's mother after all that talking she did. She was extremely shocked, and this news was still unbelievable to her.

Gween had been out of sight, out of mind for the past couple of weeks. She had been hiding since she got the results and found out she was pregnant. This was something she did not plan to tell anyone.

Otis had booked the Hampton Inn Jacksonville Beach/Oceanfront for the weekend. It was a place Gween had never been to and could not wait to see what all the hype was about. For him to spend three hundred and sixty-nine dollars a night, that bitch better have a full, on-site spa.

Otis texted Gween the location and told her to check in at three o'clock, and that he would be late. He was coming straight from work, and with the traffic on the highway, he would get there around six p.m.

It was a sunny day in March in Jacksonville, Florida. Gween walked to the balcony and took a seat in the purple lounge chair. Her view was awesome and breathtaking. She had stayed in many hotels, but never one with such an amazing view. The ocean was an amazing view, along with the crystal white sand on the beach. Gween was in heaven sitting out back, taking all this in.

Suddenly, her phone rang. She reached for her phone inside of her purple lace bra. It was Resha calling.

"Hey, bitch," Resha said.

"What is going on with you? How have you been?" asked Gween, acting normal.

Resha laughed.

"The question is, where have you been? I have called you over a dozen times, and you ignored me! We just get MIA and think it is OK not to call your bestie and let her know your sour pussy ass is OK?" snapped Resha.

Gween rolled her eyes.

She knew for the past three weeks; she had been MIA. She hated she had done that to her best friend, but at the end of the day, she needed the time alone to process what was going on. This was not something she could sleep on. She had a future growing inside of her, and it was one she must care for.

"I am sorry, bae. I needed to breathe and come to terms with the fact I am carrying a child," explained Gween.

Resha took a deep breath and exhaled into the phone.

"Well, did you at least tell him? I mean, have you stepped to him about a plan?" questioned Resha.

Gween sucked her teeth. She could not understand why she was asking this dumb ass question.

"Resha, I just told you I have not talked to anybody at all. I been to myself, bae. I have been alone, thinking," replied Gween.

Gween got up and walked over to the bar inside the room, next to the nightstand. She reached for a Corona and then paused.

Do I want to drink this and risk the chance of my child having a problem?

She took her hand off the beer and closed the bar. She slowly walked over to the bed and plopped down on the bed.

"Well, I am just asking, so don't bite my damn head off," joked Resha.

She laid on her back for about five minutes, then

turned to her side. For some reason, lying on her back was uncomfortable to her now, so the safest place was on her side. She lay there and stared at the wall until she slowly drifted off to sleep.

****

"Gail! Baby, where are you going?" yelled Jackie.

Gail had packed her overnight bag and was now heading out her front door. She was determined to find the underlying cause of what was going on in her marriage. It had been eight weeks and the doctor had removed her stitches from the C-section. Gail was furious and wanted to know why Otis had been dodging her. Why had he been taking all these extra shifts, knowing she'd just had a baby?

"I am going to Jacksonville, Florida, to see what Otis is really doing up there! Please do not try to stop me!" cried Gail.

Jackie raced in front of her daughter to try to stop her. She threw her hands in front of her daughter's face.

"Wait a damn minute. You are doing no such thing! Haven't I taught you better than this?" demanded Jackie.

Gail froze in her tracks. Right now, her mom was standing in front of her with her hands up. She did not want to be disrespectful toward her mama, so she paused.

"Mama, just let me see what is going on. You said

you were here to help me, so why are you trying to stop me? I am not going to start any trouble."

"Baby, there is a better way to handle this than to make yourself look like a damn fool!" yelled Jackie.

Jackie snatched her daughter's keys from her hand and placed them on the hood of Gail's car. She looked at her daughter, standing there, crying, and she looked pitiful.

"Baby, have you been getting any sleep at all? You have bags under your eyes, and your hair needs to be washed," Jackie said, rubbing the side of her daughter's face.

Gail knew what her mom was saying was correct, but she also wanted her husband home with her. She had not washed her hair in over a week. She had been up all night with the baby, dealing with her kids and trying to keep Otis happy. These past couple of weeks had really taken her for a spin, but all she was focused on was Otis.

"Mama, are you telling me this because I am dumb, or what? I am confused. What other way is there?" asked Gail.

Jackie took her daughter's hand and led her to the front porch, then she sat her in the white folding chairs and took a seat next to her. She reached for her daughter's hand, then she looked her straight in her eyes. She knew her daughter was beyond lost and depressed just by seeing the blackness in her eyes.

"Listen, why don't you try going to marriage counseling? See if that can help you and Otis. I know that is something you do not like to hear, but baby, why don't you try that first?" asked Jackie.

Gail looked at her mother and glanced at her front door.

Why am I going to Jacksonville to make a whole fool of myself? Why don't I just step over to my husband and ask him? He has not lied to me before.

Gail looked out at the street in front of her, then looked down the street. She wanted to see her husband's car so badly. She missed him so much. Lately, he had been distant from her. Gail just wanted her husband back, the one who loved her, no matter what, and loved the way her curves sat on her body. This new guy was awful, heartbreaking, and downright nasty.

"How can I get a man to go to counseling with me when I cannot even get him to touch me?" cried Gail.

Jackie reached her arm around her daughter's shoulders and gave her a hug.

"Oh, baby, I am sorry. Mommy is sorry," Jackie whispered.

Gail sat there, sobbing in her mother's arms. If nobody else understood what she was going through, her mother did. Her mother thought it was just Otis's cheating, but with Gail telling her this, she saw it was deeper than she expected.

NINETEEN

Otis unlocked room 273, grabbed his bag from the floor and went inside. It was now seven forty-two p.m., and due to traffic, he was an hour late getting to the resort. He knew that was going to happen so that was why he instructed Gween to go early and check in. He did not want to go looking for another place that late at night. He knew Jacksonville, but not to the point of being out late at night, looking for shit.

Otis got to bed and stopped. He saw Gween stretched out across the bed, snoring from here to China. He smiled.

Otis walked through the 2500 sq. ft. suite and went straight to the bedroom. He walked over to the bed and sat next to Gween, who was asleep, lying on her side. Then Otis rubbed the side of her face and she moved.

"Wake up, sleepyhead!" teased Otis.

Gween blinked, glanced up at him, then shook her

head. For some odd reason, she was extremely tired. She gave Otis a look when she opened her eyes.

"Well, damn, you must have been coming from up top, you so damn tired. Are we going to get some dinner?" Otis asked.

Gween heard dinner and her eyes popped right open.

"Yes, I want Long Horn Steak House," answered Gween.

Otis shook his head and smiled.

"Can I ask you a question?" Otis coughed.

Gween did not like the sound of that. She had a bad feeling and knew where this was going.

"Well, I hope I don't have to give you any blood!" joked Gween.

"Look, I owe you an apology for not telling you that my wife was pregnant," blurted Otis.

Gween got up from the bed and then walked over to the chair and took a seat. She was now facing Otis, who was still sitting on the bed.

"You are right. You never told me you had a wife who was expecting, nor did you tell me it was now!" Gween said angrily.

Otis laid back on the king-size bed and grabbed his

head. He knew he had fucked up by not telling her the truth from the jump.

"I know you are mad at me, but hear me out," he pleaded.

Gween crossed her hands across her belly. Instantly, she thought about the baby and removed her arms.

"You must understand, me and her are not on good terms. I cannot tell you the last time I had sex with her. She disgusts me, baby. She has had five kids."

"FIVE WHAT!" screamed Gween.

Otis knew he had said the wrong thing by her reaction.

Otis glanced at Gween, who had sat up in the bed and was now staring at Otis.

"Say what?" questioned Gween.

Otis looked away from her and toward the balcony view. The ocean was as peaceful as it could be. He wanted to run and jump in the ocean and never come back.

"Look, you lied to me from day one. You not single; you have a whole family, plus you just had a baby. Why are you here and not home?" Gween asked.

Otis blinked, then took a deep breath.

"I am here because this is where I want to be! I am tired of my fat ass wife. I am tired of crying. I go home every day and all I think about is you! I want to be with you. Why? I do not know," Otis said.

Gween's mouth dropped. She was in shock at what Otis had just said.

How could he hate the woman that gave him kids? Gween thought.

Gween got up off the bed and walked over to the chair at the desk. She took a seat in the chair and then placed her focus back on Otis. She wondered if she should tell him what she had in the oven. Was it even important right now and he just had a baby?

"I do not know what to say because this was supposed to be a fling, not anyone catching feelings or messing up shit," blurted Gween.

"A fling? I know that, but just a fling?" Otis said, confused.

"Yes, exactly that, a fling. You knew you had a wife, plus she was expecting, yet you still let your dick control your actions," commented Gween.

What is wrong with this girl? Why do I feel like she is trying to drop me?

"I am not going to take that as an insult, but I am sorry. I do not want you to feel like that. A fling? I hear ya!" begged Otis.

Gween's stomach growled. She was tremendously hungry now. Her belly started turning flips.

"Can we go grab a bite to eat? I am extremely hungry. We can finish talking at dinner," suggested Gween, rubbing her stomach.

Otis smiled.

He was hungry. He had not eaten since he would Door Dashed some Krystal's at lunchtime earlier that day at work. It was way beyond time for him to eat again, but food was not what he yearned for. He was ready for some of her sweet juices that she hid between her legs.

"Sure." Otis chuckled.

"What is so funny? Why are you laughing at me?" asked Gween.

Otis stood up, walked to the bathroom, and went inside. He walked over to the shower and turned on the warm water and mixed in a little freezing water. Then he took off his work shirt and looked at his body in the mirror.

Look at all that sexiness, Otis thought.

"Babe, are you coming to join me?" Otis blurted from inside of the bathroom.

He waited to hear something from her. He stood there for about five minutes before he decided to go out and check on her. He walked out of the bathroom and paused by the side of the bed. Gween had made her way back to bed and was now sleeping.

Otis looked at Gween and smiled. She looked beautiful laying there in the bed, sleeping. Otis stood there, taking in the beautiful sight of her. He stood there for about ten minutes, just staring, admiring her beautiful brown skin. Her stomach was not fat like Gail's, but it was a little plump.

Otis shook his head. The last time he was with her, she did not have a bump on her stomach.

He shook his head and walked back into the bathroom. After all, he still needed to shower and order Door Dash. His plan was to get a shower, and by the time he was out and dressed, his food would be almost there.

TWENTY

Gail looked at the phone number that she had taken out of her husband's phone. She wanted to know who "Star" was and why her husband had this number in his phone. She looked down at the number she had taken a picture of with her phone. It had to be local, because of the area code.

It was a dark and gloomy night. Gail was sitting out back on the patio that she and Otis had custom-built a few years back when they first purchased the property. Everything was still brand new, and the picture they had hanging on the wall was still intact. It was still a beautiful sight sitting on the outback in the dark.

It was after nine p.m. now and all her mommy duties were done, so she took this break to herself, trying to figure out some things. Her mother was still inside the house, putting the baby down for his nap, so Gail took this as an advantage. She wanted to make this phone call alone, without her mother around. She dashed out back once she saw her mother heading to Carlton's room to try to put him down for the night. It was late and it was time for him to close those pretty blue eyes.

The skies were full of stars, but Gail could not find one shooting star. She was sure looking for one to make a wish on. Gail had let her mother talk her into staying home, instead of going to Jacksonville, Florida, and making an ass of herself.

After her mother calmed her down, she cooked her family a small dinner. Gail was no Betty Crocker, but she could easily put together a bag meal. She had recently started taking cooking classes online to make sure she was not messing up a beat in the kitchen. Over the years, she realized she needed to learn how to cook.

Gail watched YouTube and learned how to cook homemade mashed potatoes. The menu she cooked were steamed broccoli and corn, baked chicken, cabbage, and bacon, and then for dessert, she made cheesecake. Everything she had prepared this evening was her first time cooking it. It must have been exceptionally good because at dinnertime, everybody ate it all. Not one person complained about dinner. The boys were more excited about the cake than anything. They gobbled their food down, then raced for the cream cheesecake.

Gail smiled as she watched her kids eat the cake. They did not know in less than one hour; Mama had learned how to make the cake.

Gail took a sip of her wine and sat back in her chair. Her heart was beating super-fast. At this very moment, she was beyond afraid.

A part of her wanted to call this "Star" character and go ham on her, but as a lady, she had to be calm if she wanted answers.

Gail took a deep breath, then exhaled.

She looked at the back door, then down at her phone. It was time.

Gail dialed Star's number.

Instantly, the phone rang.

"Hello, you have reached Gween, please leave me a detailed message, and I will think about calling you back," the voicemail said.

Gail's heart dropped. Her voice sounded like she was about twenty something.

"Hello, my name is Gail, um, I am calling to see what..." Gail froze in the middle of her message and hung up.

What was that? Why am I nervous? She is the one sleeping with my husband.

Gail decided to send her a text message instead this time.

Hey, when you have time, can you please call me? My name is Gail, and my number is 555-4589. I am looking for Star?

Gail sent the text, then leaned back in the patio chair. She was not expecting a reply right now, but at least a phone call. She was anxious to know what was going on.

Beep!

Gail jumped when her phone beeped!

She immediately glanced down at her phone. It was her cousin, Monay. She was not who she wanted to see calling her or who she wanted to talk to. She ignored the text.

"Baby, what are you doing out back in the dark?" a voice came from the dark.

Gail slowly got up from the chair and looked in the direction the voice had come from.

She smiled.

It was her daddy!

"Daddy! I am so happy to see you!" Gail exploded.

She had no idea her mom had called her dad. She loved her daddy more than her mom; she was a daddy's girl. Ever since she was a baby, it was always daddy this and daddy that. She never called her mother for anything. Jackie was there, but to her daughter, Jack was the shining star.

"You thought I was going to let my baby girl have her fifth child and I not show up?" asked her father.

Gail smiled, then she slowly took a seat back in the patio chair. It was beyond exciting to see her father. The last time she saw her father was Thanksgiving when the family was all together.

"Daddy, I knew you were coming, I just did not know when," joked Gail.

Jack glanced at his daughter, then took a seat next to her. He continued to examine her and could not believe this was his baby girl sitting next to him. What had Otis done to her?

"Baby, are you getting enough sleep? When is the last time you had your nails and feet done?" he asked, looking down at his daughter's feet.

Gail glanced down at her feet. They were ashy and she had dead skin around her toenails. Her feet looked like she had worked with no shoes all her life. They were awful and needed major attention.

"I am going to take care of myself, trust me, I am. I just had a baby, Dad," Gail said.

Jack shook his head and was about to say something.

"You two cannot be trusted! Why are you back here in the dark? Only the devil works in the dark," joked Jackie.

Everybody laughed.

Jackie went and squeezed between her husband and daughter.

"Honey, why don't you girls go out in the morning and get your spa day on," Jack said.

Jackie loved the idea of her husband sending her on a spa day.

"Wait a minute, so you are going to watch all your grands since you are sending me and Ma away?" asked Gail.

Jackie laughed.

"Now, don't you have that woman that comes and helps you? She can come to help me. I may have it, but it's been a while since I've been left alone with a newborn," explained Jack.

"My point. I will have Shelia on standby, so just in case you need help, she will be ready," explained Gail.

Gail knew her mother had already told him about Otis, and she was just waiting for him to ask.

"Baby, I just put Carlton down. I am going to take a shower and get ready for bed myself. It has been a long day for both of us," Jackie said as she stood up.

Jack followed and stood up with his wife.

"You guys go ahead. I will be inside in a few, just make sure you do not wake any of them bad boys," joked Gail.

Her parents laughed.

Gail's phone buzzed. It was a text message.

She waited until her parents were inside the house before she looked at the message.

Hey, I really don't know you nor did I give my number out to anyone! Who are you looking for? This is Gween's phone, not Star.

Gail glanced at the message again.

So, who is Star? Who is Gween?

Gail looked at her phone for about twenty minutes, not knowing what to reply. It was a mistake. *Did he have the wrong name by the number? What is going on here?*

Gail looked confused. She did not want to text the wrong person about her husband. She wanted to reply in a way to know for sure Otis was with this woman.

Can I ask you something about my sister's husband?

Gail looked at the text for ten minutes, then she deleted it. It just did not sound right to her. She needed something else to say, but what could she say? She was out of ideas on what she could say, so Gail sat there, thinking about what she could say to this stranger.

TWENTY-ONE

Gween sat across the table from Otis. They were dining at the Juicy Crab for their dinner. Gween was asleep when Otis took his shower and woke her when he was out and fully dressed.

Gween had woken up when there was a knock at the door. She jumped out of her sleep and then realized she had drifted back off. She was furious at Otis for not waking her up. She jumped up, showered and, in no time, she was ready. Otis laughed at how fast she moved.

"I see we made it!" chimed Otis.

Gween looked at Otis and gave him an awful look. She was still mad because they could have missed their reservation Gween had made for dinner.

"Your ass ordered Door Dash, so you did not want to eat out," joked Gween.

Otis playfully laughed.

"Can I take your order?" the host said, walking up.

"I already know what I want. I will take a combo

number 3 with lemonade, light ice, three extra corn, four extra eggs, mild seasoning, and please hold the pepper," Gween said.

Otis's mouth dropped to the table. He could not believe she had ordered all that and not one item was for him.

"Sir, what can I get for you?"

Otis examined the menu and did not know what to get. He had never been there, so he searched for something that stuck out for him. He glanced down and saw combo number 18 with fish and shrimp.

"Combo 18, fix it to the recipe," suggested Otis.

The host smiled and wrote something down on her pad, then she retrieved the menus and politely walked away.

Gween stared at Otis.

"Why don't you take a picture?" joked Otis.

Gween tossed her napkin across the table, and it landed right in front of Otis.

"I cannot help it, you're sexy as fuck!" gloated Gween.

Otis knew this girl was crazy and that was what he loved.

"Question?" Gween said.

Otis froze quickly, with a surprised look on his face. He knew she wanted to finish talking about Gail and the baby, something he did not want to deal with at all. He had come on this trip to get away, not to bring the drama.

"Why didn't you tell me from the beginning that, one, you are married, and two, you had a baby that was due any minute?" questioned Gween.

Otis glanced over at Gween, looking her right in the eyes. He saw she was serious, but also, he saw a glow. Her face was shiny, makeup was on point, and the lip color she picked was a cool red. She was stunning in his eyes.

"Look, I know you said you wanted me to be honest, but who knew we were going to end up still kicking it," responded Otis.

Gween looked at him, shook her head and bit her bottom lip. She could not believe what he was saying.

"So, why did you tell me about the baby now? What changed?" asked Gween.

More than anything, she wanted to know why he waited so long to tell her what was going on. A baby was nothing you hide. No matter how hard you try, you just cannot hide a child.

Otis shifted in his chair. This was a subject he did not want to talk about, but from the looks of it, he had no choice.

His chair was on fire, and he was slowly burning.

"Look, I did not come on this trip to explain what my home life is about," replied Otis.

"You think you are going to play me? I want to know what is going on, Otis," demanded Gween.

Otis sucked his teeth, then slowly turned his head to examine his surroundings.

"Are you going to answer me or what?" blurted Gween.

One thing Otis did not like was for a female to think she could back him in a corner. The situation was already on fire and the more steam that Gween lit, the shittier Otis felt.

"I am not about to break down to you what I have going on at home! I told you already that I am not happy at home," blurted Otis.

"Listen, I do not care what and how you feel about your wife, but at the end of the day, you at least owe me the courtesy of telling me the truth," Gween said.

Otis was about to say something when Gween's phone rang.

"Go ahead and answer it," Otis snickered.

Gween looked at Otis and could not believe he just

snickered at her.

What was so funny, or what tickled him so bad?

Gween pushed silent on her phone and ignored the call. Whoever was calling was not more important than the conversation she was having right now.

"You don't want to get your phone?" asked Otis.

As soon as he said that a text came in. Gween wanted to curse Otis out so badly; it took everything in her to compose her posture. Besides, they were out to eat, and making an ass of herself was something she did not do.

"First off, please lower your tone. Whoever is calling is not important. Their number not even saved in my phone, so, back to the question," demanded Gween.

"What do you want to know?" asked Otis.

"So, in under five minutes, you have forgotten what I asked you?" questioned Gween.

Otis threw his head back, then smiled at her and crossed his arms. He did not want to explain this shit, but from the look on Gween's face, it was the best he did.

"OK, you want the truth? OK, I am married and my wife just had a baby boy about two months ago. Me and my wife do not agree completely, and we have not slept with each other since she found out she was pregnant. I do live with her and our five kids," explained Otis.

157

Gween leaned back in her chair, took a deep breath, then exhaled.

What did I just hear? Gween thought.

Otis stared at Gween, waiting for her reply. He was just as lost for words as she was.

"You… I mean, you did not think I needed to know this. We have been slurping each other down the past few months, and not one time did you tell me you had a family. I am lost for words on that part. Do you plan to stay with your wife? asked Gween.

"I do not want to be with my wife. I am tired of the crying and shit going on. Plus, my wife is not like she used to be. She is pushing close to three hundred and fifty pounds. I am not into BBWs at all. Her sexiness has faded away to me," confessed Otis.

Gween's phone lit up with text messages and voice mail. She looked at the message and blinked.

"What are we?" asked Gween.

"I would love to try to get to know the real Star in my life," joked Otis.

Gween smiled, but it was not the kind he was used to.

"That sounds great. I also have something to tell you," confessed Gween.

Before the couple could say anything, their host came back to their table with their orders.

"Hello, here are the combos for you, sir, and madam, here is yours," the host said.

"Thank you," they both said.

The host left the table.

"What is that?" asked Otis.

Gween put her bib around her neck to connect it. She was starving and could hardly get the bib to go around her neck due to her wanting to start eating so quickly.

"Slow down," Otis said.

Gween had already put a slice of potato in her mouth by that time. Suddenly, she spat it out in her hand, then looked at Otis.

"Damn, this shit is spicy as fuck," complained Gween.

Otis laughed.

"I know just by what you're telling me about your wife, that you have a lot of shit you're dealing with at home." Gween spoke in between stuffing her face.

Otis nodded.

"I really like you, Otis. I am serious, but I am not going to get my heart all jacked up because you feel you are undecided on what you want," Gween advised.

The rest of the night, they ate their combos in silence. Neither of them had anything to say to the next.

Otis thought hard on what he wanted to do about Gail. He knew leaving her would be that day he's waiting for, but how would he go about it? He was feeling Gween and was ready to leave his wife.

Gween sat there, eating her seafood. She wanted to blurt out that she was pregnant, and what they were going to do about it. She needed answers, and right now was not the right time because how was she going to tell him? From the looks of it, he did not want any more kids.

TWENTY-TWO

Gween glanced down at Otis as he slept the Saturday morning away. They had a late Friday night out and Otis wanted to sleep in, so Gween did not want to mess with him. They had ended the night with a bang! Legs, arms, and every other part of the body you could name were thrown in the air. Everyone was satisfied. Both had given the next their best love.

Gween examined Otis laying naked in the hotel bed with just a t-shirt on. The way he lay with his hard dick out made Gween's pussy wet. His body made Gween go crazy for him, and those brown eyes. Out of his work clothes, Otis was built like 50 Cent, the rapper, with a lighter skin color. His arms are enormous, like he was a pro wrestler. The arms did not drive her so much up the wall as his body did, though.

Gween smiled, then she folded her hands and stared at her future baby daddy.

After about ten minutes, she took a seat in the

comfy brown chair that was right next to the bed. Gween looked at the clock on the wall; it was forty-five minutes after eight a.m. Damn time change has everybody all messed up, because right now, it would be at least 10 a.m.

Gween reached for her hot pink iPhone from off the nightstand. She wanted to send Resha a good morning text and see what she was up to. Gween went to her inbox and paused. She was so caught up in Otis and herself, she forgot about the text from the weird number. She scrolled down to the text message and read it slowly.

Hey, can you give me a call? It's about my husband, Otis!

Gween blinked. She looked at her phone, closed out the text message, and sat back in the chair. She stared at Otis.

She was shocked. He'd just told her about the wife and now she was texting her. I wondered what he told her. *Why is she texting me? And who gave her my number?*

Slowly and quietly, she walked toward the bathroom, peeking behind her to make sure Otis was still asleep. She then closed the door and sat on the toilet bowl. She looked at the message again and blinked harder. Her mouth filled with saliva, and her head started thumping from getting upset about the text. There was a sting in her stomach, then it growled, and she was ready to eat. She rubbed her belly, then leaned back on the toilet.

Gween sat there with a puzzled look on her face. She did not know what to do or say to this lady because, in the end, she was wrong for sleeping with a married man. No matter how she put it, she was wrong.

Gween took a deep breath while staring at her phone. Gween went back to the message and hit reply.

Hey, this is Gween, not Star. Give me a reply!

Gween sent the text.

She rubbed her belly and shook her head. She was ready to see what was going on behind closed doors. Something didn't sound right, and all she wanted was the truth. She also wanted to know why her name was Star?

Gween's phone vibrated. She jumped and looked down at her phone, then became extremely nervous.

This lady did not even reply; instead, she called.

"Hello?"

"Hi, this is Gail. I saw you just replied to my message from last night," Gail said.

Gween took a deep breath, then rubbed her belly. Her tummy was ready for breakfast, and she knew it. Gween leaned over just a little bit to her right-side wall, to try to get up off the low toilet.

"Hey, yes, I am just seeing your message about your husband, but my name is not Star," answered Gween.

"Mmmm!" replied Gail.

"Excuse me, what does that mean?" mumbled Gween.

"I am trying to see why he has your name under Star. It is clear you know my husband because you are still on the phone with me," blurted Gail.

Gween took the phone away from her ear and looked at it, then placed it back on her ear.

"Who do you think you are yelling at? Listen, bitch, you don't know me, and trust me, baby, you don't want to get to either," acknowledged Gween.

There was a brief silence on the phone, then Gween heard kids playing in the background.

Gween frowned.

"Is that his family?" asked Gween.

"What is it to you? Not like you care. You have my husband not even wanting to come home to us," snapped Gail.

Gween peeped out from the bathroom and Otis was still sleeping. She closed the door back and took a seat on the toilet.

"Look, my name is Gween, and I had no idea he

164

had a wife until you had the baby. He was with me in Savannah around the time," explained Gween.

Gail cried.

"Please don't cry. I don't want you to think I am the bad person here, but I had no idea," continued Gween.

Gail finally caught a grip and stopped crying.

"Is he there now? You know our baby is not even two months old yet? He was born February 13th. Don't you think he should be home with his son?" cried Gail.

Gween grabbed her head and thought about what his wife had just said. So, they had been talking for about three months, and that meant she was pregnant already and he had plenty of time to tell her what was going on.

"Look, I just want to know what I am not doing? I love my husband. We have been together for over eight years," asked Gail.

Gween looked down at her left hand and it was shaking.

"What do you want me to do? I am not a sour female, so all the beefing, I am not with it and do not care for it," answered Gween.

Gail was quiet.

"Hello?" Gween said after a brief silence.

Gail was still quiet.

Gween looked at the phone, and the timer was still rolling so she was still on the line.

"Are you going to say something?" asked Gween.

"I am shocked! Out of eight years, never have I cheated on my husband. I never even thought about another man. I am in love with Otis and Otis only," chimed Gail.

"What are you saying?" asked Gween.

"I do not know what to do. I have never been in this situation before," answered Gail.

"Do you want answers? You want to know what is going on?" asked Gween.

"Honey, I been asking and trying to see what is going on," replied Gail.

"OK, can you come to Jacksonville today? We can meet, all of us, and Otis won't know," suggested Gween.

"I just had a baby, and if I try to leave, my mom will be on my ass. Can you come here? Is there a way you can get him to come home? We live in McIntosh," replied Gail.

Gween thought about that for a second.

Did she want to help Gail? Was it worth it? What was in it for her?

"OK, I will be there today. I know how to get him to go home," replied Gween before ending the call.

Gween was beyond speechless. Since when did she care about a bitch's feeling? What was wrong with her?

Gween walked over to the bathroom mirror, glanced down at her phone and then back at her belly. She was really feeling Otis, but was it to where she would play second fiddle? What about his wife? *What will she do when she finds out I am having his baby too?*

TWENTY-THREE

Otis pulled out of the parking lot of the resort. He was beyond mad at how he'd just wasted his money for the weekend, but only spent one night there. The resort would not refund him any of the money, either. Otis was extremely angry at Gween and the hotel. The least they could have done was give him half the money back if anything.

Otis thought about what Gween had said. She said she had an emergency and needed to get to Resha. For some reason, that did not sit right in his head. He had spent plenty of time with Gween, and when she was unreachable then that is just that. She does not want to hear from anyone. So, what happened to Resha?

Otis reached for his phone as he stopped at the red light under the overpass. He dialed Timothy's number and waited for him to answer.

"Hello?" a sleepy voice said.

"Wake your ass up. I need to know something.

Have you spoken to Resha today or last night?" asked Otis.

"Man, I have not talked to Resha in about two days now. I been calling her number, but no answer," answered David.

Otis wondered if he was overreacting.

Maybe she did have an emergency and just did not want to tell her what was going on. It was a lie.

"What is going on with you and Gween?" asked David.

Otis waited a few seconds before he replied.

"I am, I mean, she is OK. We were supposed to spend the weekend with each other, but she had an emergency so that was canceled," Otis said sadly.

"Well, don't sound all pooped out, my guy. She will call once everything is OK," answered David.

Suddenly, Otis's phone beeped with an incoming call. Otis glanced down and saw it was Gail calling.

"I am OK. I am on the way to the hell hole now. "I swear I did not plan on going home," whined Otis.

David laughed.

"Bro, you just had a baby! Who wants to be home with all that fucking crying?" joked David.

Even though he was joking about the situation, Otis really hated going home. The thought of going home made him want to call into work and get an extra shift. He would do anything not to spend any time with his wife.

"I guess you and Gail cooking Saturday dinner today," David joked.

Otis hung up the call. David knew he hated it when he joked about him and Gail. Otis really hated being with his wife. Over the years, her weight change had turned him off in so many ways.

Otis got on 95 North, heading home. He cut on Avant's "Separated" and turned it all the way up. He wanted to ride home in peace and not think about Gail or what was going on. If Gween was not calling, he did not want to talk to anyone at all.

****

Gween stayed three cars behind Otis's car. He thought she had left way before he did, but she parked outside the resort at the gas station. She saw Otis come down and get into his car and pull off. The entire time she trailed him, from the time he pulled onto the highway.

Gween had lied to Otis and told him she had an emergency and they needed to cut their mini baecation short. She grabbed all her things and headed out the door, leaving him lying in the bed, naked, with a hard dick.

Gween pulled onto the highway, the fourth car in

170

line. She stayed a good distance behind Otis, so he could not see her.

Gween pulled out a Black & Mild from her armrest. She glanced down at it, then she tossed it back in the armrest and felt for a pack of Trident gum. She found the pack and took a piece. She did not have time to stop and grab food since she had to keep up with Otis.

Gween looked down and realized she was pushing eighty miles per hour just to keep up with the red car so that meant Otis was doing about ninety-five miles an hour on the highway.

Gween pushed the call button on her steering wheel.

"Call Resha."

Her phone started calling Resha.

"Pussy hoe, where you at?" Resha said as she answered her phone.

Gween laughed.

"Bitch, let me ask you this. Would I be wrong for setting up Otis?" asked Gween.

"Come again? What you mean, bitch?" joked Resha.

Gween got over in the far-left lane when she noticed Otis was getting over. Now there were two cars in between her and Otis at this point.

"I am serious! His wife contacted me, and I am on the way to their house in McIntosh!" replied Gween.

Resha made a choking noise and then coughed.

"Say what? Bitch, since when do we help the wives? Oh no, hoe, you different!" Resha whispered.

Gween laughed.

"Bitch, he's the one lying to me. Re, she just had a baby boy, and they live in the same house," Gween informed her.

"This is shitty. So, Mr. White Teeth's 50 Cent looking ass has been lying to you? Did I understand you right?" Resha asked.

"Correct."

"Plus, his wife just had a baby boy?" asked Resha.

Gween did not say anything. She thought about all of this.

I expose him, then where does that leave me and my baby? Will he still help me with the baby? Wait a minute, I have not even told him about the baby.

"Wait!" hollered Gween.

"What is up? Are you OK? Something happened?" Resha asked quickly.

"I expose him, right, but I have not even told him about the baby. So, where would that leave me?"

172

questioned Gween.

Resha got quiet and thought about the question.

"I think you should think about this. How do you know she is just not playing you so he can leave you alone?" suggested Resha.

Gween was with her homegirl on this one. What if her doing this messed up her chance of having a family with him? This was her first baby, and nobody was going to make her fail as a mother.

"The ball is with you, homegirl, so what are you going to do?" Resha asked.

Gween did not have an answer because she had been blindsided by this. She was only concerned about him lying to her and not telling her the truth. But in the end, what about her once he finds out she is pregnant?

"Fuck it, Resh, I am going! I must go. I already told her I was coming," whined Gween.

Resha coughed.

"Handle what you need to, and please share your location with me. Just in case I need to pull up on somebody," Resha said.

Gween laughed.

But she knew her girl was serious about the

location. She knew with the situation she was going into, anything could happen.

"OK, trick. I am sending it as soon as we get off the phone," answered Gween.

Gween pushed the red cellular button on her steering wheel and ended the call.

"Share location with Resha!" Gween said to her car.

"Sharing location now!" her car replied.

Gween turned up her radio and cruised behind the two cars, making sure she did not lose sight of Otis's car. She really wanted to pull over and grab some food because she was starving but she did not want to lose him. So, once again, she decided to stay on the highway. His wife was waiting. She had already told her she was coming, so what would she look like, going back on what she already agreed to?

Gween shook her head.

TWENTY-FOUR

Gail made a simple breakfast that morning for her crew. She made a fruit bowl, toast, and one fried egg. She was supposed to make a big breakfast for her kids since it was Saturday morning. Gail normally cooks pancakes, bacon and toast. That was her special dish she made every Saturday for her crew. This was a meal her family anticipated on Saturday; it was tradition.

"Mom, everybody has eaten, can you please take them to the park? Me and Carlton will be OK here alone," suggested Gail.

Jackie looked at her daughter, then at her husband. Something was not right with her, and mommy bear was on it.

"What is going on with you? Suddenly, you changed. You were crying all night and now this morning, you are cooking breakfast. You do not even cook," Jackie said.

Gail laughed.

"Mom, I am OK!" pleaded Gail.

Jackie looked at Jack, and he nodded.

"OK, I guess we will get the boys rounded up and head to the park," replied Jackie.

Gail smiled to herself.

Jack and Jackie got up from the kitchen table and made their way to the boys' room. Jackie gave Carlton to Gail as she got closer to her.

"Take the prince," joked Jackie.

Gail took her son and walked into the living room. She took a seat in Otis's head chair. His all-time favorite game watcher was a La-Z-Boy. She and Carlton got in the chair, and she reclined her feet, then laid back in the chair.

Carlton stared at his mommy, then he smiled.

"Mommy's man has a pretty smile," Gail said playfully.

Gail reached for her phone, looking at the notifications for a second. Still no call from Otis; not even a missed call or text.

She frowned.

Gail looked down at her son, and tears ran down her cheeks.

"Mommy is trying to get Daddy to come home. I

am trying my hardest to fix whatever I messed up," she cried.

Baby Carlton watched as the tears came down his mommy's face.

She looked down at her son and shook her head.

"Mommy, are you coming too?" asked PJ.

Gail quickly looked up, wiping her face to answer her son.

"No, you, G-ma, and Papa go and have all the fun!" Gail said excitedly.

All her boys raced to the front door behind Papa.

"Dad, you sure you can manage all these energized small people?" asked Gail.

Jack laughed, then he was out the door with his grands, waiting for Jackie to come on.

Gail smiled at her father. She knew her boys were in good hands, and they could handle them, she just loved messing with her father.

"Now, I am taking your key with me. I don't want to get any phone call about you in Jacksonville with my grandson," Jackie stressed.

Gail knew fussing with Jackie was not a winning situation. Her mom would go on and on, so she didn't waste her energy on that.

"Mom, you are right! I am OK, you can take the damn key. Hell, take the house key as well," joked Gail.

Jackie looked at her daughter and blinked. She saw her daughter was doing OK last night, but why? What made her so jolly? Someone must have called her and explained something. Last night, her daughter was too crazy to leave, and today, she told them to go out with the kids.

Jackie walked up to ger grandson and gave him a kiss on his forehead. Then she slowly turned her head and glanced at Gail, then back at Carlton.

"Nana loves you, CC," Jackie said.

Gail smiled when she heard the name.

"CC!" repeated Gail.

Jackie walked out the door and ignored what her daughter asked.

Gail waited until she heard them crank up their car and was out of the driveway.

Gail laid Carlton down and reached for her cell phone. She called the mystery woman, Star. She wanted to make sure they were still on for her coming by today.

The phone rang.

"Hello?" she said.

"I was just making sure you were still on for

coming over to talk," inquired Gail.

"I am on my way," replied Gween.

Gail ended the phone call and sat back in Otis's chair. She looked over to the car seat where Carlton was. He was fast asleep, smiling from ear to ear.

Gail wondered what had his attention to the point he was smiling.

As she thought about it, her eyes got heavy. Next thing you knew, she was slowly falling asleep. No matter how hard she kept rocking, it only slowly closed her eyes.

****

It was now three forty-five and Otis had just pulled down the street to his house. He had driven like a bat out of hell to get off the highway. Otis hated driving on I-95 or any other highway, to be exact. Driving on the highway made his heart rate go haywire.

Otis pulled up in his driveway and noticed Gail's car was gone. It was Saturday, so it went nowhere unless it was a family thing. He checked his text messages to see if he had missed anything. There were no texts from his wife besides the old ones from before he left work Friday afternoon.

Otis grabbed his bag and got out of his car, headed toward his front porch. He retrieved the house keys from his front pocket and made his way inside his home. As soon as he got inside, he stopped.

There, lying with their feet up on his couch, was Gail. On the right side of her was Carlton's car seat with him inside, sleeping his life away. Otis looked toward the stairs to see if he was going to hear his boys.

Gail pulled her leg down off the arm of the chair, then scooted back in the chair. She wiped her eyes and looked directly at Otis.

"Oh, you made your way home. I have been calling you," explained Gail.

Otis did not say a word. He did not have the energy to fuss with Gail at this point. He just wanted to get some sleep and prepare for work Monday morning.

"I am not going to fuss with you. I am home now, so please do not come with this mess," explained Otis.

Gail slid forward in the recliner, then she got up from the chair and walked over and stood right in front of Otis.

"You had fun? Were you happy with her?" Gail asked.

Otis looked surprised.

What is she talking about? What does she mean by "did I have fun"? Or if I were happy with her?

Gail bit her bottom lip. She did this when she got nervous and felt like she was being bombarded.

Otis was about to answer her question when their doorbell rang.

Otis looked at the front door, then back at Gail.

"You are expecting company?" Otis asked.

Gail walked past her husband with a confused look on her face. She was expecting Star to come in with him, but it looked like she had flaked.

"Who is it?" yelled Gail.

Otis turned around and looked at the front door. He had just come from outside and nobody was out there with him.

Mmm, Otis thought.

Gail opened the door, took a step back, then turned her head and looked at her husband.

"Please don't go upstairs, I believe this is your guest!" Gail said, smiling.

Gail took a step back from the front door and let the estranged guest inside.

Otis turned around and looked at the door.

"What in the hell!" Otis whispered to himself.

He could not believe what he was looking at. Why was she in his house?

Otis's mouth dropped to the ground.

"Oh no, baby, pick it up. It is not time for that," explained Gail.

Gween walked inside with the same yellow and white dress Otis saw her dash off in. Gween looked at Otis, then turned and shook Gail's hand.

Otis was nervous at this moment. Sweat dripped down his back, forehead, and across his nose. When Otis was unsure of something, he started to sweat.

Why is Gween here with my wife? Why is my wife smiling? Why do they act like they know each other?

Otis's whole chest stung with pain. Every deep breath he took in, his chest hurt more. Suddenly, his ear rang, his right leg shook, and he had no idea why his body was reacting like that.

Gail stared at her husband and noticed his appearance. He was shaking and breathing extra hard. She counted his chest movements.

It is about to be a madhouse, Gail thought.

TWENTY-FIVE

Gween kept her eyes on Otis, who appeared to be a sweat box. He had sweat pouring down his forehead heavily. Gween almost wanted to smile at him, but she did not want to set him off.

"OK, Gail, you asked me here, I am here, and so is your husband," Gween blurted.

Gail joined her husband and tried to put her hand on his back, but he pushed her away.

Gween spun her head; she wanted no parts of that fire.

"How did you get her number? Did you go through my phone?" asked Otis.

Gail put her hand on her hip, smiled, then turned to Gween.

"I texted Star. That is the name you have it under. She informed me that her name was not Star, and that you were with her," stated Gail.

"What are you getting at? Why are you texting

people? Why are you starting trouble?" asked Otis.

"How is she starting trouble? All she did was ask me a question. She was not disrespectful at all," answered Gween, looking at the couple.

Otis sucked his teeth.

"You two bumping pussies?" he said softly.

Neither lady heard what he said, but he was dead serious. *Why is Gween taking Gail's side for, anyway? This shit just doesn't sit right with me, and I think I am being set up.*

"I did not call her with any drama. I thought she was going to come at me with it, but we talked," replied Gail.

Otis put his hands on his head and looked away at Carlton sleeping. He would do anything to be in his spot right now. He was sleeping away all the drama that was going on, sleeping like a prince.

" I would like to know if you have had unprotected sex with my husband?" asked Gail.

"Do not you dare answer that stupid ass question! Why does it matter to you who I am fucking? We not fucking!" Otis exploded.

Both ladies turned their heads and stared at Otis.

"Why are you making this a big deal? You told me

184

you don't want your wife; she is fat and your house is not the same. It seems to me this lady loves you, so Otis, tell me what is going on at home, and do not say the baby," Gween asked.

Otis could not believe Gween had taken sides with his wife. *Since when were they buddies?*

"Otis, look at me," begged Gail.

Otis turned and looked at his wife.

"What?" asked Otis.

"Every fucking time I turn around, you're pregnant, and you gain so much weight!" yelled Otis.

Both ladies looked at Otis.

Baby Carlton shuffled in his car seat. His eyes slowly opened, and he smiled as he looked around.

"Please, you already woke up the baby," Gail said as she walked over to the car seat.

"Are you tired of Gail? Is that your name?" Gween asked.

Gail nodded.

"Are you just upset about her having kids or what? She is no whale," joked Gween.

Gail laughed.

Otis was done playing fools with these two.

"Gween, I thought we had a connection. I see you

let my wife poison you into doing, what is this called? I was about to leave my family. Well, I was thinking about it, but you dried that plan up," Otis said.

Gween laughed.

"Say what? You were going to leave your family? You are a dirty bastard," Gail said, crying.

"Stop all your fronting, bitch. You knew this was ending when you hit over three hundred pounds. This is all your fault, Gail, so do not even try to tell me otherwise," Otis explained.

Gween could not believe that Otis was cursing at his wife like that. It was clear he called her bitch often.

"I can be out of our house, but can you afford this alone?" blurted Otis.

"Just stop!" Gail yelled.

Carlton cried. Gail cried harder, picking up her son.

"Who are you yelling at?" Otis demanded to know.

"That is your wife, why are you treating her like you do not know her? You keep calling her a bitch. How can she be a bitch, but you have a family with her? She just had your son, and you're calling her a bitch? What is wrong with you?" Gween asked.

Otis was not even embarrassed by what Gween said. All desires to fix what he had with his wife were long gone.

"I am ashamed to say that I love you, Otis. I know I had five kids, but I did not make them alone. You can help me help myself," begged Gail.

Gween saw Gail was begging her husband. *What is wrong with them?*

"You are going to take him back and beg him to straighten up?" Gween asked, confused.

Gail looked at Gween and wanted her to leave now.

"Thank you, Gween, for coming out today and speaking with me. Can you leave now? Me and Otis, we must talk about something," cried Gail.

"What did we accomplish? Nothing. He still hasn't admitted to anything and I would love to know why he lied," blurted Gween.

"Lower your tone in my fucking house. Matter of fact, you can leave," Otis said, walking to his front door.

"Oh, so we going to act like that? OK, just last night, you were eating my pussy and ass," Gween said.

Gail gasped for air. She could not even think straight.

"Say what? He told me he does not eat pussy. Since we have been married, I'd never had him do any of that with me," Gail said.

Otis tried to grab Gween's arm, but she snatched back.

"Do not put your lying ass hands on me," blurted Gween.

Gween stepped out of Otis's reach.

"Look, I do not know what you plan on doing by telling my wife these lies, but you have done enough," Otis said.

Gween smiled. She knew he was going to act like she was the bad guy. They were still married to each other.

"Gain? Come again, nigga? Because when you met me, I was on my shit, and still am," answered Gween.

"Y'all, please, the baby is awake," begged Gail.

"It is funny you mention the baby is awake," Gween said as she reached for something in her back pocket.

"Please don't shoot!" yelled Gail.

Gween cheesed harder.

"Shoot you for what? I did not come to your house for all of that. I am not a violent person, I am just here for the truth," Gween explained as she pulled out some papers from behind her.

"Look, whatever you have, I do not care. You have done enough," demanded Otis.

Gail took Carlton out of his car seat, bouncing him

up and down on her shoulder to calm him down. He heard his father yell, and it upset him tremendously.

"Well, I suggest you start telling your wife that you about to be a father again!" blurted Gween.

Gail's knees shook, and she quickly placed Baby C back in his chair. She turned around and stared at Gween, who held papers with a smirk on her face.

"Let me see that," snapped Gail.

"No, leave her alone with her fake shit. How can she be pregnant when I never had sex with her?" explained Otis.

"You really going to say you never had sex with me? OK, so how about we go back to the hotel rooms, or better yet, ask your best friend, David!" Gween said.

"David? You mean David from out of town?" Gail asked.

Gween smiled and shoved the paperwork in Gail's face.

Gail examined the paperwork.

"How long did it take you to conjure up this story?" Otis asked.

"You really think I can fake a pregnancy? You claim you real, but it looks like that was a lie," answered Gween.

"Shut up! Stop lying to me, Otis! How does she know David?" asked Gail.

Otis did not answer.

"Are you sure it's his baby? I mean, you saying David, but you could have heard him talking to him," explained Gail.

Gween laughed harder.

"You know what, I was already prepared for all this shit! He can see me in court when the baby is born. I feel sorry for you, lady. It's clear as day your husband does not want to be here with you, but you want it to work out?" asked Gween.

Gail threw the papers at Gween.

"Just get out!" Gail yelled.

Gween picked up her papers from the floor, then walked to the door. She turned around and looked at them.

"You two are made for each other! Nigga, you will never see my child. Bet your ass on that!" she yelled.

Gween walked out the door. She raced to her car and got inside. Eyes filled with tears, she slowly cranked up her car. Never in a million years did she think she would have his baby too.

Gail looked at her husband, then back at her son.

"What were you thinking about? Now you have

another baby on the way?" Gail asked.

Otis huffed.

"I am sorry! I never meant to hurt you," explained Otis.

"Bottom line, you did, so now what am I supposed to do? The baby is coming, dumb ass!" yelled Gween.

"What can I do but take a DNA test? If the baby is mine, I have to do what I have to," pleaded Otis.

"But you don't even spend time with us and now you have a whole new child? What am I supposed to do, sit back, and watch you cater to this woman and her newborn?" Gail asked.

"No, I am not asking you to do that. I am asking you to stand behind me. I made a mistake, and I am sorry, Gail," cried Otis.

Gail looked at her husband, then started crying. She loved Otis with all her heart, but this was something she did not feel they could come back from. A child and a whole new life? How could her family compete with that?

"One question! Did you ever stop to think what you were doing was going to come out? Did you even stop to think about AIDS?" Gail asked.

"What are you saying?" Otis asked.

Gail looked around her house, then back at her son.

191

"Otis, I want you out! Grab your clothes, shoes, whatever you need, but you must leave," cried Gail.

"You say what? Are you throwing me out? What about my kids?" pleaded Otis.

Between the tears, Gail smiled.

"Now, you have kids?" she said.

"I have had kids, and I have had a wife. I am sorry, Gail, but you do not want me out," Otis said.

"Baby, I do! I am filing for divorce first thing Monday morning. I would rather raise my boys alone than to have you humiliate me," answered Gail.

Otis looked at his wife's eyes and realized they were a cold gray, not the pretty, shiny green he was used to. He wiped away his tears and slowly made his way upstairs. He was terrible hurt. Never did he think his wife would leave him.

EPILOGUE

One year later…

It was now a year later and Gween had given birth to an 8-pound 8-ounce baby girl named Selena. Gween had managed to have a healthy pregnancy and was enjoying being a mom. This past year had been rough for her since she had been a single parent. Otis was living in Brunswick GA in his own apartment. Gail managed to finally let his ass go after cheating. About three weeks ago, Gail asked Gween to take a DNA test. She wanted to know if her ex-husband had fathered a child outside of their marriage. The past year has been killing her, simply because she wanted to know the truth. Gail loved her husband to death and was considering working things out with him. But there was no way she was going to do that if he had fathered a baby with another woman. Today was the day the results was being read.

"Mommy loves you, Selena," Gween whispered.

193

Selena smiled.

Gween picked up her child's pink and purple car seat and walked to Gail's front door. She was back here at this same house where she learned Otis was nothing but trouble. She walked up to the door with her child and knocked.

"Who is it?" a lady asked from the other side.

"Gween!" she replied.

The door opened.

"Hey there, how are you doing? Is that Selena?" Gail asked as she let Gween inside.

Gween walked by Gail and made her way to the living room chair. She put Selena's car seat on the chair next to her.

"Yes, this is my precious Angel" Gween said.

Gail walked over to them both sitting down and stood in front of them. She watched as Gween reached over to pick up Selena.

Gail's heart started to beat fast. She could not

194

believe how beautiful the baby was. She has so much hair, plus she was as chubby as could be. Gail wanted to hold her. She wanted a daughter so badly but never had any luck.

"Oh lord she is gorgeous!" blurted Gail.

"How's Carlton?" Gween asked right before saying, "Thank you!"

Gween looked over at Gail and could see a difference. For one, she had lost some weight. That little tummy she had was now gone. Her nails were done and her hair was in a ponytail. She had upgraded since the last time they saw each other.

"He's upstairs with my mom; he's doing okay!" Gail answered.

"Have you spoken to your husband? I mean I know you have. I have not," mumbled Gween.

Gail took a seat next to Gween and stared her straight in the face.

"I have spoken to him, I mean, we have five kids together, so we have talked," Gail said.

Gween took a deep breath as if she was annoyed. Otis had been giving her the cold shoulder. The truth was, he really hadn't seen Selena face to face yet. The last thing Gween wanted to do was get into that with Gai. She was here for one reason and that was the results.

"Okay I understand," lied Gween.

Gail reached for the brown envelope on the table in front of them.

"The results came in. I haven't opened them," Gail said.

"Why not? What you mean you haven't? You could have!" Gween exclaimed.

Gail gave Gween a shocked look. She didn't want to open the results without her being there. Last thing she wanted was to be accused of some shit.

"Okay, well, are we waiting for Otis to come?" Asked Gween.

Gail smiled. She had already called and told Otis his ass had to be there. This was his mess, and he was not leaving her alone while fixing this.

Suddenly, the front doorbell started to ring.

Gween's heart started racing. Since it had been a long time since she saw Otis, she wasn't sure what her reaction would be when she saw him. She tried to calm herself down. She didn't wanna act like a fool in front of Gail or her baby girl.

Gail got up and made her way to the front door and she opened it.

Otis stepped inside looking good as always. He was dressed down in all white, with some black Nike boots on. He had a white and black Nike snap back on his head.

Gail saw her husband and had to restrain herself from hugging him. Otis pulled some roses from behind his back, smelled them and then gave them to Gail.

"For my pretty lady," Otis said.

Gween rolled her eyes and sucked her teeth while keeping her composure. She just wanted this to be over so she could get back to her life. She wanted nothing to do with Otis.

"Can we just get the results out the way? I have

some where to be," Gween said when she noticed the two of them were giving each other seductive stares.

Gail took the flowers from her husband and placed them on the table.

"Go ahead, Gail. Read the results," Otis snapped.

Otis just knew this was not his baby and wanted nothing to do with Gween or the baby. For all he knew, Gween could have been pregnant before he smashed her. Gween was getting impatient and was just about ready to go.

"Can we just get this over with?" Gween asked, looking at her watch.

"Why don't you just leave?" snapped Otis.

Gween rolled her eyes as she grabbed Selena's baby bag, attempting to get up.

"Wait a minute," Gail said, opening the brown envelope.

The room got quiet, and it was now the moment the group was waiting for. Gail stood there with the papers in her hand, glancing at them.

"Otis, um, you are the father of her child!" she cried.

"Told your stupid ass," Gween yelled.

Otis stood there disappointed and ashamed that he had made another child. Gween looked at Gail who now had tears running down her face. She felt sad for Gail. She was hurt and most of all her husband betrayed her. Gween picked Selena up out of her car seat and turned toward Otis and Gail.

"This is Selena," she said.

Otis looked at Selena. Her eyes were just like PJ's, and she was chubby just like Jr. was. At this point, there was truly no reason to continue to deny her. She indeed looked like his boys. Otis blinked his eyes and turned toward Gail.

"Baby, I'm sorry, I am," Otis said.

"I am sorry I didn't believe you," Gail managed to say, turning her attention to Gween.

Gail knew Otis wanted to make things work between them, but another child was just something she couldn't do. Otis had been trying to win her back for the past six months. She thought she would eventually give in, but now that she knew the results, she decided to stay divorced and continue to co parent.

"Baby, I am so sorry for putting you through this," Otis cried out.

"Otis, don't be sorry to me. Be sorry to that precious little girl that you've been denying all this time."

He didn't say much. He looked at Gween then Selena and walked over to them.

"I'm sorry and if you don't mind, I would like to co parent. I also would like my boys to meet their sister," Otis said, shocking Gween and Gail.

Although things weren't going to end up the way Otis wanted them to, he figured he had put these two women through enough. Yeah, he wanted his wife back, but the ultimate betrayal happened, and he lost her forever. That was just going to have to be something he dealt with. As for Gail, she couldn't get past Selena being here. She knew it wasn't the baby's fault, That blame lay on her husband, and he didn't deserve to be with her. Gween had already known Otis wasn't shit, and he didn't have to be in

200

Selena's life if he didn't want to. One thing, she wasn't going to do was beg him. She looked at Otis and gave him her new number. Then she looked over at Gail.

"I would love for the boys to meet their sister when you're ready."

Once Gween said what she wanted, she grabbed Selena and made her way out the door. Gail looked at her with a half-smile before she spoke.

"Okay, no problem. You have a good day."

Gween left out of the door, not turning back. Otis and Gail decided to sit and have a talk about the new arrangement with the kids. They loved each other very much, but at the same time, being together just wasn't in the cards for them.

THE
END

Made in the USA
Monee, IL
23 May 2023

34383037R00114